"Suppose," I said, looking gloomily at my reflection in the mirror in Nesta's bedroom. My hair was a frizzy mess. I had an aloe-vera mask on that made me look like a ghost and a big spot threatening to erupt on my chin.

"Lack of self-esteem," said Izzie. "That's your problem, T. J. You are a babe, but you don't know it. Look, you have fabulous hair that you always scrape back in a plait, long *long* legs that you never show, a fab figure that you hide in baggy tracksuits, and a great mouth that all those thin-lipped models who have collagen injections would die for."

Always one to accept compliments graciously, I said, "Humphh. And you clearly have the observational skills of a brain-dead gnat."

Mates, Dates, and Sleepover Secrets

Cathy Hopkins

Simon Pulse

New York   London   Toronto   Sydney   Sing

First Simon Pulse edition September 2003

Copyright © 2002 by Cathy Hopkins
Originally published in Great Britain in 2002
by Piccadilly Press Ltd.

SIMON PULSE
An imprint of Simon & Schuster
Children's Publishing Division
1230 Avenue of the Americas
New York, NY 10020

Designed by Debra Sfetsios
The text of this book was set in Bembo.

Printed in the United States of America
10

Library of Congress Control Number 2002117224

ISBN 978-1-4424-1421-1

For Rachel

(And thanks to Rachel, Grace, Natalie, Emily, Isobel, and Laura for letting me know what's hot and what's not. And thanks to Jude and Brenda at Piccadilly for their input and for giving me a chance to be fourteen again. And last but not least, thanks to the lovely Rosemary Bromley.)

Chapter 1

Noola the Alien Girl

"'We are the champions, *we are the champions*,'" sang some Stupid Boy outside the window of the girls' locker room.

"How sad is that?" asked Melanie Jones as she rubbed strawberry-scented body lotion onto her legs. "We beat them three weeks running and they win *once* and think they're it."

"Yeah," I said as I pulled my hair back and plaited it. "Today," I said, raising my voice so that Stupid Boy could hear outside, "was a mere blip in our team's otherwise excellent performance."

"Yay," chorused the rest of our team, who were in various states of undress after the soccer match.

"You woz rubbish," shouted Stupid Boy.

I shoved my stuff into my sports bag and stepped outside into the dazzling June sunshine. There was Stupid Boy—namely Will Evans, goalie from the boys' team.

"You talking to me?" I asked.

Will tried to square up to me, which was difficult, seeing as I'm five feet seven and he's a squirt at five feet four.

"Yeah," he said to my nose.

"In that case, would you mind using the correct grammar? It's you *were* rubbish, not you *woz*."

Will went red as the group of guys around him sniggered.

He stuck his tongue out at me.

"Oh," I yawned. "Like I'm *really* scared now."

By now, most of the girls' team had finished changing and had come out to see what was happening. It was always the same. Every Saturday, after the match, the games continued off the pitch— often with the girls bombing the boys with balloons swollen with water from the locker room taps.

I picked up my bag to go home. I'd got bored with it all in the last few weeks. I was sure there had to be a better way to get a boy's attention than splattering him with water.

Anyway, it was Saturday and that meant lunch with Mum and Dad. Dad insists that we eat together as "a family" on the rare occasions that he's not working. What family? I think. It's not like I have hundreds of brothers and sisters. Only Marie who's twenty-six and left home to live in Southampton years ago and Paul who's twenty-one and been away studying in Bristol.

"Oi, Watts," called Will.

"The name's T. J., actually," I said, turning back.

"T. J.? What kind of name is that?" sniggered Mark, one of the other boys on the team. "T. J. *T. J.*"

I tried to think of something clever to say. "It's *my* kind of name," I said, for want of anything better.

I didn't want to get into the real reason. I'd never hear the end of it. My full name is Theresa Joanne Watts. Like, yeah. How dull and girlie is that? But Paul has called me T.J. since I was a baby and it stuck. Much better than Theresa Joanne. But

I wasn't going to explain all this to the nerdie boys from St Joseph's High. If they knew I hated my real name, then that's what I'd be called for ever.

"Okay then, *T. J.* You and me," said Will, pointing at a picnic table by the football pitch. "Over there. Arm wrestling."

Now this was tempting. Arm wrestling was my major talent.

I took a quick look at my watch. I had time.

"Okay, Evans. Prepare to die."

We took up our positions opposite each other at the table and both put our arms out, elbows down. A small crowd soon gathered round as we grasped hands.

"Ready," said Mark, "steady, GO."

I strained to keep my lower arm upright as we began to arm-wrestle.

"Come *on*, T. J.," cried the girls.

"Come *on*, Will," cried the boys.

"Hey, T. J., there's a guy looking for you outside the boys' locker room," said Dave, the boys' team captain as he came out to join us.

"Nice try," I said, not looking up. I wasn't going to break my concentration for the oldest trick in

4

the book. Plus, Dave was A Bit Of A Hunk and I usually said or did something stupid when one of his super species was around. I made myself focus. The crowd around was beginning to get excited as I kept my arm firm and Will's started to weaken.

"Show him, T. J.," said one of the girls.

I could feel my strength wavering as Will fought back and my arm wobbled. Then I summoned every ounce of energy and *slam*, Will's arm was on the table.

"Hurrah," cheered the girls, then they began singing. "*We* are the champions. *We* are the champions. Champions, the champions, champions of Europe."

"*Stupid* girls," said Will, rubbing his hand and going to unlock his bike. "Anyway, we won the footie and that's what really counts. So there."

"Oh, grow up," I called as I walked away.

"There really is someone looking for you, T. J.," said Dave, catching up with me and putting his hand on my shoulder.

As I turned and looked into his denim-blue eyes, my stomach went all fluttery.

"I didn't say it to distract you. Over there, see?"

he continued. "Hippie guy with dark hair and an earring."

I looked to where he pointed and there was my brother Paul, a short distance away.

"*Nihingyah*," I said to Dave, who looked at me quizzically.

I shrugged and turned back toward my brother, who gave me a wave. No point in explaining, I thought, as I made my way over to Paul. Dave would never understand how I get taken over by Noola the Alien Girl when confronted by Boy Babes. She doesn't know many words. Mainly ones like *uhyuh, yunewee,* and *nihingyah*, which I think means, "oh, yeah," and "thanks," in alien-speak.

"Hey, T. J.," said Paul, giving me a hug.

"Hey," I said, and hugged him back.

"Bit old for you, isn't he?" taunted Will as he rode past on his bike.

"Get a life, you perv," I said as I linked with Paul and drew him away from the crowds. "He's my *brother*."

Paul grinned and looked back at Will. "Looks like I'm interrupting something."

"As if."

"Come on, you can tell me. Someone special?"

"Only the local pond-life," I said. "You home for lunch?"

"Yeah," sighed Paul, and ran his fingers through his hair. "Bad vibes. Thought I'd escape awhile and come and find you."

"Scary Dad still mad with you?"

Paul nodded. "And some. The way he goes on, anyone would think I'd committed a murder rather than dropped out of university. But you know how he is."

Boy, did I know! Night and day, me and Mum had to listen to him going on . . . and on: Paul has ruined his life. Paul has spoiled the opportunity of a lifetime. Paul has wasted his talent. If only Paul were more like Marie. He was always a dreamer. He had it too easy. What's to become of him? Where did we go wrong?

On and on and *on*.

See, Dad's a bigwig hospital consultant. Mum's a GP. Even my sister, Marie, is a doctor. Plan was, Paul was to join the club, follow in the family footsteps sort of thing. Only he never wanted to.

He wanted to be a musician. He went along with the doctor bit. Got good grades. Got into medical school. Did a year. Did a self-awareness type weekend in London. Saw the light or something. Dropped out of college. Grew his hair. Started spouting self-help jargon. Got into alternative medicine and rejected pretty much everything Dad stands for. Oops.

Dad mad.

Mum sad.

Me, though, I'm glad. Not that he's having a hard time, of course. I feel sorry for him getting all the stick from Dad, but Dad's got me lined up to be a doctor as well. Ew, no thanks. Way too much blood. I want to be a writer, so I'm hoping all this with Paul will pave the way for my eventual fall from grace.

"Seriously though. Looks like you had a lot of admirers there," said Paul, pointing back to the football pitch.

"Nah," I said. "Boys are never interested in me."

"Looked to me like they were *very* interested."

"Only because I'm the arm wrestling champ," I grinned. "I had to show them what's what after we lost at footie this morning."

Paul gave me a look and sighed. "T. J., you're impossible. Wake up and smell the hormones, kiddo. You're easily the prettiest girl on the team."

"Me, pretty? Yeah, right. Get real."

"I am," he said and pulled on my plait.

"You're only saying that because you're my brother."

"No," he said. "You're always doing yourself down. Like you can't see that you're gorgeous."

"Now I know you're kidding. I couldn't get a boy if I tried."

"Have you tried?"

I shrugged. "Er, dunno. Not really. But . . . it's like, I either talk alien or go into my Miss Strop bossy act and start correcting their grammar. I mean. D'oh. How flirty is that? Or else, I terrify them with my super-human strength. You know, humiliate them by winning at arm wrestling. Very girlie. Not. It just never seems to come out right."

"It will, T. J.," said Paul gently.

"But *when*? Most girls in my year have sore lips from snogging. Me? The only sore bits I've got are bruises from where some boy has kicked me in a soccer game. I'm hopeless. Hannah was so good at the boy thing. They used to really like her."

Paul looked at me with concern. "Sorry about Hannah. Mum told me. When did she go?"

"Fortnight ago," I said as my eyes stung with tears. I was still feeling raw about her leaving, but I was determined not to cry like a baby in front of Paul. Hannah was my best friend. And she'd just gone to live in South Africa. Yeah, in South Africa. Not exactly the kind of place you can hop on a bus to when you fancy a chat. I was missing her like mad.

"You'll soon find new friends," said Paul.

Arghhh. If another person says that to me, I think I will scream. In fact if Paul wasn't my brother, I'd have socked him. People don't understand. *"You'll soon find other friends,"* like you can go out and buy one in the supermarket.

"I don't *want* new friends," I said. "I want Hannah back."

Hannah was a riot. A real laugh. I knew I'd never meet anyone like her ever again. It was her that came up with the nickname Scary Dad for my father. And with her around, boys never noticed I was tongue-tied or awkward—she babbled enough for both of us. I could hide behind her and they never realized that my cool was actually frozen shy.

As we turned into our road, we almost ran into Mr. Kershaw on the pavement in front of us. He was walking his dog, Drule. Or rather Drule was walking him. Drule is a big black Alsatian and Mr. Kershaw was having a hard time holding on to the lead.

"He can't wait to get to the park." He grinned as Drule yanked him forward.

I laughed and turned to go in our gate but Paul stopped me.

"Actually, T. J., don't go in yet. I didn't just come to walk you home. I've got something to tell you."

"What?"

As he shifted about on his feet, something told me that I wasn't going to like what he had to say.

Chapter 2

Giggling
Girlies

"Hey, T. J.," called Scott Harris from his bedroom window. "Hang on, I'm coming down."

Before I could answer, his head disappeared and the window closed, so I sat on the front step outside our house and waited for him. The Harris family has lived next door to us ever since we moved here when I was seven, so Scott is the next best thing I have to a brother besides Paul. Scott's two years older than me and lately has discovered girls. Or rather, girls have discovered him. He's cute in that Richie from Five kind of way and there's often a group of giggling girlies outside his gate. Scott liked to talk his latest conquests over with me and no doubt that's what he wanted to do now.

"T. J.," called Mum from inside. "Lunch'll be on the table in five minutes."

"Coming," I called back. "Just got to see Scott for a mo."

I was glad Scott was coming over, as I badly needed someone to talk to. I was hoping he'd distract me from the sinking feeling in the pit of my stomach. Paul had just told me that he was going traveling with his girlfriend, Saskia. For a year, maybe two. Starting with Goa, then maybe Australia and Tahiti. First Hannah, now Paul. What was going on? My two favorite people disappearing out of my life in less than ten days.

"Where've you been?" said Scott, appearing round the rhododendron bush in our front garden.

I opened my mouth to say "football," but he was off again before I had time.

"Been looking everywhere for you."

"Good," I said. "Because *I* want to talk to you."

"Why? What's happening?"

"Oh, everything," I began. "You know Paul dropped out and everything, well, now he's off traveling. Hannah's gone. I—"

"Really? Cool," said Scott, looking at his watch.

D'oh? I thought. No. Not cool. "Scott, are you listening?"

"Yeah. Course. But I need to ask a favor first."

I sighed. "What?"

"Hot date," said Scott, with a grin. "I need to borrow a fiver. Just for today. I'll give it back to you next week when I get my allowance."

Yeah, I thought, you said that last week when I lent you two quid. But then I didn't want him to think I was a cheapskate. No one likes a cheapskate. I was sure he'd give it back to me in the end.

I rummaged around in my sports bag, found my purse, and pulled out the fiver pocket money that Mum had given me that morning.

"Thanks," said Scott. "You're a pal."

"So who's the sad victim this afternoon?" I asked.

"Jessica Hartley. She's from your school."

I nodded. I knew Jessica all right. She was hard to miss. Just Scott's type, glam and girlie with long blond hair.

"Yeah. She's in the year above me. In Year Ten. Anyway, as I was saying, Paul's leaving tomorrow,

Hannah's gone and it feels like . . ."

"Actually," interrupted Scott, "talking about your school. Do you know Nesta Williams?"

"Yes," I said. "She's in my class."

Scott looked as though he'd won the lottery. "Wow. You're kidding. How *fantastic*. She's like, a five-star babe. Could you put in a word for me?"

For some reason this irked me. Who did he think I was? First the bank that likes to say yes, now a dating agency?

"What about Jessica?" I asked.

"What about Jessica?"

"Well, if she's your girlfriend, would she like you asking about Nesta?"

"Hey. Not my fault," said Scott with a wide smile. "So many girls, only one me."

My jaw dropped open, but then I realized he was joking. At least, I *think* he was joking. Sometimes he acted as though he believed he really was God's gift to women.

"Oh, poor you having to share yourself around us miserable impoverished girls," I said.

Scott laughed. "You know, you're really cool, T. J. You're so easy to talk to. Like one of the boys."

"Thanks," I said, feeling chuffed with the compliment. Easy to talk to? Maybe that was it. I didn't need to worry about being tongue-tied or saying the wrong thing. I don't need to talk, only listen. Maybe there was hope for me after all.

"Anyway—Nesta. What's she like?"

It was out before I could stop myself. "Oh—a complete airhead."

I felt a bit rotten saying that, as I don't really know Nesta beyond the fact that she's the prettiest girl in the whole school. I've never spent any time with her.

"Airhead's okay," grinned Scott. "It's not like I want her to *talk* to."

"Yeah, right," I said, suddenly feeling miffed. Maybe it *wasn't* such a compliment that I was easy to talk to? Oh, I don't know. Boys. They confuse me.

"Wanna arm wrestle?" I asked.

Scott looked at me as if I was out of my mind. *"What?"*

"Arm . . . oh, nothing," I said as I saw Jessica tottering up the road in strappy high heels. "Your date's here."

Jessica appeared at the gate and looked surprised to see me. She looked fantastic in a tiny white tank top and white jeans with diamante bits sewn up the seams.

"Hey," said Scott, leaping up and going over to her. "You look good."

Jessica was staring at me as though I'd just crawled out from under a stone.

"Thanks," she said and jerked her thumb at me. "Sister?"

"Next-door neighbor," said Scott. "You know each other from school, right?"

I smiled at Jessica, but she didn't smile back. "Can't say I've noticed her," she said. Then, flicking her hair as if dismissing me, she turned away.

"See you later," winked Scott. He put his arm round Jessica, snuggled into her and whispered something in her ear.

Jessica giggled and they disappeared off down the road.

"Er . . . nice to meet you, too," I called after them.

Huh, I thought. You can act as superior as you like, Jessica Hartley, but I know Scott's got his eye on someone else. One week and you'll be history. So there. Stick that in your diet yogurt and eat it.

I sat out for a bit longer. So much for my heart-to-heart with Scott. Paul was leaving and I felt miserable. Who could I talk to? Scott was a waste of time.

"T. J.," called Mum's voice. "Lunch. On the table. *Now*."

As I got up to go in, I saw Mr. Kershaw and Drule go past again. Mr. Kershaw was jabbering away to Drule and the dog was looking up at him as if he understood every word.

That's it, I thought. I'm going to ask Mum for a dog. She said I could have a pet ages ago. A best friend of the furry kind. One who won't leave the country.

Why didn't I think of it before?

e-mail: Outbox (1)
From: goody2shoes@psnet.co.uk
To: hannahnutter@fastmail.com
Date: 9 June
Subject: Norf London blues

Hi Hannah

Miss you loads.

Idea: Why don't we run away to L.A.? I can write film scripts and you can be a dancer?

Bad news: Our team lost at footie. But then, you were our best player so I guess it's to be expected. Don't your parents realize the devastation it has caused nationally by removing you from the country?

My bro, Paul, is leaving. Off to Goa. With Saskia.

Ag. Agh. *Agherama*. I'm losing all my friends.

Scary Dad is in v bad mood. It's not *my* fault Paul wants to play the bass guitar and be a hippie instead of being a doctor. Atmosphere at home awful.

Good news: Beat that scab Evans at arm wrestling. Hahahaha.

Mum says I can have a dog. Suggest you get one too if your mum will allow until you settle in at school. Dog—man's best friend etc, etc. We're going to go next weekend to look for one.

Paul is staying the night. Hurrah. And for Sunday lunch. After that he's off and I will be All On My Own.

And guess what? Jessica Hartley from Year Ten is going out with Scott. But he fancies Nesta Williams. Hahahaha.

If another person says, "You'll soon make new friends," I vill 'ave to keell them.

I am starting a collection of made-up books by made-up authors. For example:

Medical Hosiery by Serge Icklestockings
Modern Giants by Hugh Mungous
Please send contributions.

Tata for now

T. J.

PS: Confucius say: Man with no front garden look forlorn.

---

e-mail:	Inbox (1)
From:	hannahnutter@fastmail.com
To:	goody2shoes@psnet.co.uk
Date:	9 June
Subject:	Cape cool

Hasta banana baby

Miss you too, megalooney.

Keep your chinola up. It's hard for me too. Everything's so differentio here. It's supposed to be winter but it's hot hot HOT. Cape Town is mega. You must come and visit. So far been up Table Mountain. Pretty cool. Though hot. Haha. And to the beach. Pretty hot though cool. Haha. There are loads of beaches here, everyone hangs out there. Boys here look more healthy than back home. All suntans and white teeth. Still stupid though if the one next door is anything to go by. His name's Mark. He's okay but he asked me to a barbie at his house and he eats with his mouth open and you can see all his food. Ew. Gross. He'll never get off with anyone if he doesn't learn to eat properly.

Book titles. Hmmm. Let me think.

Okay.

Pain In the Neck by Lauren Gitis

Hahahahahaha.

Chow bambino

Love you muchomucho

Hannah

Confucius say: Who say I say all those things they say I say?

Arf. Arf.

Chapter 3

The
Wrinklies

"Stand close," said Mum as she pointed the camera at us in the back garden. "Put your hand on Paul's shoulder, Richard. And *try* and look as though you like him a bit."

Dad shuffled about behind us then finally put his hand on Paul's shoulder. "Might be more appropriate if Paul put *his* hand in *my* pocket," he muttered.

"Oh, for heaven's sake," said Mum. "Enough now. You made your point over lunch. This is our last day together as a family before Paul leaves for Goa. Try and act like a grown-up."

Paul and I tried not to laugh as Dad looked at the lawn like a naughty schoolboy. Quite an achievement seeing as he's in his sixties, but Mum can be Scary Mum to his Scary Dad when she likes. She gets a look in her eye and you know she's not to be messed with. Hannah used to call my parents the Wrinklies because they're so ancient. Mum had me when she was forty-five and Dad was fifty-three. They thought they'd finished having children with Paul. Then seven years later, along came yours truly. I think I was what is commonly known in birth terms as A Surprise. Or A Mistake. Whatever. All I know is that I have the oldest parents of anyone in school. I used to get embarrassed when there'd be all these young mums in T-shirts and jeans waiting after school, then along would come my mum or dad in their "comfy clothes" looking more like my grandparents. I started telling people that Mum and Dad were actually the same age as normal parents but they'd been captured by aliens one summer and kept as an experiment on their spaceship for two days. The trauma made their hair grow white and they grew old before their time. One girl in my class actually believed me.

Mum took her picture and Dad headed for the car.

So much for our last day together as a family before Paul's trip, I thought, as I watched Dad reverse his Mercedes down the driveway and zoom off toward his golf club.

The rest of us trooped back inside, and Paul and I began to clear the table. Lunch had been a strained affair with Dad giving me a lecture about "the importance of qualifications" and "a good career meaning a good start in life." It was so obvious it was aimed at Paul, but I tried to look as if I agreed with everything Dad said. Anything to keep the peace.

Then he started on about how much Paul going to college had cost him. What a waste it all was.

"I will pay you back," said Paul. "I really will."

"It's not the money," said Dad. "I want you to be happy."

"I will be," said Paul. "I *am*. I want to see the world. Experience life. It's going to be brilliant."

"Well, at least let me give you some decent medical supplies for the journey," said Dad.

Paul sighed. "It's sorted, Dad. Don't worry."

Dad didn't look convinced and, for a moment, I felt sorry for him. He doesn't normally look his age, but today he did. He looked sad and a touch weary. Sometimes he can't accept that people have their own plans for their lives. He's so used to people obeying his every word at the hospital, he thinks it's going to be the same at home. Poor Scary Dad. I think he means well.

After loading the dishwasher, Mum went to water the pots on the patio and Paul and I went through to the living room. Paul flopped on the sofa and began flicking through the Sunday papers. At the bottom of the pile was our school newspaper, which he began to read.

"There are loads of things you can do in here," he said after a while. "Art, drama, choir. Getting a hobby would be a good way of making new friends."

"You sound like Dad," I said, sitting next to him and stretching my legs out onto the coffee table, "organizing my life. Anyway, I have loads of hobbies. Tennis. Football. Karate."

"Sounds like you'll meet lots of boys doing that stuff, not girls."

"Don't be sexist. Girls do all that stuff as well."

"Oh, *sorry*. Didn't realize you're a feminist," he teased.

"I'm not. I just believe women are the superior race," I teased back.

"Oh, look, there's you," pointed Paul as he came across our class photo. "And Hannah."

"It was taken just after Easter," I said, looking over his shoulder. "I look awful."

"No, you don't. What are the other girls like?"

"Oh, God. All sorts." I pointed to some of the girls in the photo. "That's Melanie and Lottie. I get on okay with them. They were at footie yesterday. Those three are the brainboxes, those two are the computer nerds, Jade and Candice are the bad girls that like to bunk off, Mary and Emma are the sporty girls, Wendy's a bit of a pain."

"So, who do you hang with?"

"Well, Hannah before she went, obviously. And now I suppose Melanie and Lottie a bit, but they're a twosome really. I'm lumped in with the brainboxes seeing as I'm usually first in the class at everything. Except math. I hate math."

Paul continued to study the photo.

"Now, she looks nice," he said. "Who's she?"

"God, typical," I said when I saw who he was pointing at. "She's Nesta Williams. Only the best-looking girl in our school."

"She looks like that girl in Destiny's Child."

"Beyoncé."

"Yeah. So who are her friends?"

I pointed out Lucy Lovering and Izzie Foster.

"They look like fun. Tell me about them."

"Not much to tell. I don't know them that well outside school. They don't do football or any of the stuff I do. Inside school, they're sort of in the middle. Popular. Not too swotty, not too disruptive, though Izzie does ask a lot of questions in class sometimes. One teacher called her Izzie 'Why?' Foster. But *everyone* fancies Nesta, that I *do* know. Even Scott next door. She's in the drama group and I think she wants to be an actress. She's probably completely self-obsessed. Anyone as gorgeous as her has to be."

"Not necessarily," grinned Paul. "I'm gorgeous and I'm not self-obsessed."

"And *I'm* gorgeous and I'm not self-obsessed," said Mum, coming back in with a

27

bunch of white roses she'd cut. "So why don't you get in with this crowd?"

"Oh, you don't understand, Mum. They hang by themselves. They'd never let anyone as boring as me in with them."

"You're not boring," said Mum, taking the newspaper from Paul and scanning the back page.

"Don't bother to read that," I said. "It's completely out of touch and dull."

"Well, here's your chance to change it," said Mum, handing it back to me.

"What do you mean?"

"There, back page. I saw it the other day when I had a look through. I thought you might be interested. It says that they're looking for a new editor, seeing as the old one will be moving on at the end of the year. And they want to make it more of a magazine than a newspaper. Applications open to everyone from Year Nine upward. You only have to do eight pages or so as an example."

"Not interested," I said, putting the newspaper back on the pile of papers.

"But you want to be a writer," said Paul. "You

28

should go for it. It would be good practice."

"Nah, people think I'm a swot as it is. If I went for that, they'd only hate me more."

"Suit yourself," said Mum and began to root around in the cupboards for a vase. "But I see that Sam Denham is doing a talk for all those interested."

"Sam Denham? Where does it say that?"

"Ah, so suddenly it's not so boring." Mum picked up the newspaper and read from the back. "Monday, eleven June, four thirty in the main assembly hall. That's tomorrow. He's going to talk about journalism. It says he got started on his school magazine."

Sam Denham is a celebrity journalist and though he's old, at least in his thirties, he's still cute in that Ricky Martin kind of way. They always have him on the news when they want an opinion about anything. He always has something interesting or funny to say.

And he's coming to our school?

"Maybe I *will* go to the talk," I said. "But only to listen."

```
e-mail:      Outbox (1)
From:        goody2shoes@psnet.co.uk
To:          hannahnutter@fastmail.com
Date:        10 June
Subject:     Night night
```

Hi Hannah

Feeling mis. Bro Paul gone. He and Saskia are booked on the overnight flight to Goa tomorrow. Boo hoo. Everyone I care about is going away.

Gotta go, school A.M.

T. J.

By the way, our crapola newspaper is looking for a new editor, and Sam Denham is coming to school tomorrow to do a talk. Apparently he got started on his school mag.

```
e-mail:      Inbox (1)
From:        hannahnutter@fastmail.com
To:          goody2shoes@psnet.co.uk
Date:        10 June
Subject:     Sam the Man
```

WAAAAKE UP.

   Exscooth me? Did you say Sam Denham as in Sam

Denham from the telly? He's a top babe. V V jealous. Wish never left U.K. Be sure to wear something short that reveals your legs as they are one of your best features. And sit on the front row.

T. J., you *must* go for editor. You'd be brilliant at it. And it would take your mind off missing me and Paul. I've read all about this kind of thing in Mum's mags. The agony aunts are always telling people to "keep busy" and "throw yourself into your work." I think this is a godsend. Your destiny.

And you think you're miserablahblah? Try being me. In a new country. With no friends at all. Not even Melanie and Lottie. No, young lady, you don't know you're born, as Dad would say.

Yours truly,

Your Agony Aunt Hannah

P.S. Few more for the book collection
Over the Cliff by Hugo First
The Cat's Revenge by Claude Bottom
Arf arf arf arf arf arf!

Chapter 4

A
Lonely Little
petunia

"I'm just a lonely little petunia in an onion patch, an onion patch, an onion patch," sang the record in my head. It was going round and round, louder and louder, as I sat eating my lunch in the school playground the next day.

I was on my own because Melanie suffers from awful hay fever and thought that sitting outside would make it worse. Course Lottie had to stay in with her to keep her company and hand her tissues. I was going to explain that as pollen is airborne, it could get anywhere, so it wouldn't make much difference where she was, but I didn't want her to think I was a Norma Know-It-All. Too many people thought that already. In fact lately I've found myself holding back when I know the answers to things in class. Let someone else be the one who always gets it right. It doesn't win you any prizes in the popularity stakes.

Perhaps I should have stayed in with them, I wondered, as I looked around at all the groups of friends. It is definitely possible to feel lonelier in the middle of a crowd than when on your own.

Most of the school was out making the most of the heat wave. Everyone in pairs or three or fours. All busy talking, laughing, having a good time. I always used to sit with Hannah at lunch, and I felt really self-conscious sitting on my tod. Like, everyone must be staring, going, "Oh, poor T. J., she's got no mates."

I continued munching my peanut-butter-and-honey sandwich like I didn't care, but I did care. I didn't like this feeling of being the odd one out.

"Hey, T. J.," called a voice near the bike shed.

I turned round to see Wendy Roberts. "Hey."

"You heard from Hannah?" she asked as she

perched herself on the bench next to me and lowered the straps of her top so the sun could get to her.

I nodded. "Yeah. I've had a few e-mails. I think she's missing England."

"You must miss her, too," she said.

"Yeah, I do," I replied, wondering what was going on. Wendy never normally gave me the time of day, so why this sudden interest in Hannah? Sensitive and caring are not words that come to mind when I think of Wendy. Mean and self-centered more like. But no one else had asked about Hannah or how I was, so maybe I'd got her wrong.

"You going to the talk tonight?" she asked. "Sam Denham?"

I nodded.

"He is gorgeous, isn't he? I saw him on morning telly last week. He was so funny. I wonder if he's got a girlfriend. Are you going to go for editor?"

I shook my head. I wasn't going to tell her, but Hannah's e-mail had made me think. Maybe I *should* go for editor. It would be perfect to take my mind off things, plus, as Paul had said, good practice for when I'm older. But I didn't want to tell

Wendy. I didn't want her thinking I was getting ideas above my station, and anyway, I might not even get the job.

Wendy got out her mirror and applied some lipstick from her bag. "Great color, isn't it?" she said. "Natural with a hint of gloss. Good for us brunettes. Want to try some?"

"No, thanks." Us *brunettes*? What is all this matey, let's-bond-over-a-lipstick act, I wondered. What *does* she want?

"Er, T. J. . . ."

"Yeah . . ."

"You know that exercise we had to do for math . . . ?"

Ah. So that was it. I felt my face drop. I couldn't help it. For a split second I thought someone was being friendly because they might have cared about me. Obviously not.

"Well I meant to . . . ," Wendy continued.

"You want to copy my homework?" I interrupted.

"Oh, T. J., *could* I? You'd be doing me the most *enormous* favor and you know what Mr. Potts can be like if anyone hasn't done it. . . ."

35

"Actually math isn't my best subject . . ."

Wendy stiffened. "It comes so easily to you but if you're going to be precious . . ."

"I'm not. Here take it," I said and got my book out of my bag. I couldn't be bothered arguing. Math didn't come easily. I had to really work at it and the last bit of homework had taken hours after lunch yesterday and I still wasn't sure I'd got it right. But I wanted friends not enemies, and Wendy could be really nasty when she wanted to be.

Just at that moment I caught Izzie Foster watching me from the bench to my right. She raised her eyebrows and half-smiled at me.

"Thanks. You're a doll, T. J.," said Wendy, grabbing my math book out of my hand. Off she went, leaving me sitting on my own again.

Izzie was still staring. She was sitting with her mates Lucy and Nesta and, like most of the other groups of girls dotted around the playground, they looked like they were having a good time, just relaxing in the sun. Nesta was at one end of the bench rubbing lotion onto her legs and Lucy was at the other with her skirt hiked high and her legs stretched out to get the sun. Izzie said something to them and they both looked over, then Izzie got up and came to join me.

"Hey, T. J. I was just thinking. You heard from Hannah?"

"Wendy's already borrowed my homework," I said.

"What homework?" asked Izzie, looking puzzled. "I saw you sitting on your own and suddenly remembered that Hannah'd gone. I wondered how you were doing?"

So people *had* noticed me sitting on my own. Well, I didn't need anyone's pity.

"I'm fine," I said, getting up and putting my half-eaten sandwich in the litter bin. "Got to go."

I was going to go and sit and read in a cubicle in the loo for the rest of the lunch break. That way no one would see me on my own and feel sorry for me.

"So, to sum up," said Sam Denham from the stage later that day, "you've got five main rules, and if you stick to them, you won't go wrong."

I turned the page of my book to write more notes.

"Rule one," he said. "Your job is to stop people just flicking through the magazine. You have to draw them in to actually read what's on the page. You do this by having hooks on the page. These are pictures, titles, words under the picture that give an idea what the feature is about, a quote and the picture captions. Now, if people scan your page, they can quickly access what it's about. So, the title and the captions should be . . . what?"

He looked around as a few hands went up in the hall, including Nesta Williams' who was sitting next to me. Sam pointed at her to answer.

"*Interesting*," she said, and gave him a flirty smile.

"Right," said Sam, flashing a big smile back at her and keeping his eyes on her for a few moments. "*Interesting*. Or funny. These hooks are as important, if not more so, than the copy."

I was scribbling furiously to get it all down when I noticed Nesta hadn't written a thing. "Do you need paper?" I whispered to her, ready to rip out a page for her.

She grinned and shook her head. "No, thanks. I'm just here for the view."

You and half the school, I thought. I don't think

a talk had ever been so well attended, not only by the girls but also by the teachers. But then, most of the teachers are aspiring writers, according to Hannah's mum. She was a headteacher before she left for South Africa. She told us that half her staff were secretly working on novels and planning to get out of teaching.

"Rule two," Sam continued. "Make sure your picture or photograph is appropriate to the copy. You don't want a big smiley picture of someone next to a tragic piece. Rule three. Use your pictures and captions in a creative way. For instance, you're doing a sports page and have a feature about tennis coaching. Any ideas?"

Wendy Roberts put up her hand. "You could have a photo of some kids playing, with the caption *Learn to play tennis*."

Sam nodded. "You could. It's apt, but not very inspiring. Any other ideas?"

I had one, but I didn't want to look a prat in front of everyone. Wendy was blushing like mad after Sam had squashed her idea. I went over in my mind what I'd say if I could only pluck up the courage.

Sam pointed at a girl at the back.

It was Izzie Foster. "How about a picture of Pete Sampras in full flight going after a ball, saying something like, 'Are you the next Sampras?'"

"Now we're cooking," said Sam. "That's more like it. Only it might be a bit intimidating, as most people know they'll *never* be the next Sampras. So, it might put them off going. But, good idea. Any more?"

Me *me*, I thought, trying to summon up the courage to put my hand up.

"Come on," said Sam, looking round at the rows of silent girls. "Part of being a pro is throwing ideas into the pot and not feeling bad when someone knocks them down. It doesn't matter. We learn as much by our mistakes as our successes, if not more. Come on, who's going to stick their neck out?"

I could feel myself going red as I put my hand up, but I was bursting to see what he thought of my idea.

"You," said Sam, looking in my direction. "Lara Croft on the front row."

I looked behind me. He couldn't mean me, could he? *Lara Croft?* But no one else had their hand up.

He pointed at me again. "You. Come on. Girl with the plait?"

Oh, he *did* mean me! I could feel myself going redder than ever. I took a deep breath. "What if you use a picture of, say, Tim Henman?" I finally managed to get out, "on his backside with the ball bouncing past and a caption saying something like, 'Even the best needs a little extra help'?"

"Love it," beamed Sam. "It may not make you want to play tennis, but it will make you stop long enough to read what's going on."

"Well done, Lara," whispered Nesta as the red from my face spread to the tips of my ears.

"Rule four. Never be afraid to try new things. Rule five. In your layout, make sure the reader always knows where to go next. And make sure the information is accessible, especially in a magazine. Know your market. And not too many long paragraphs. Break some of it up. You know, ten tips about this, five ways to do that, and so on. . . ."

At the end, he took some questions from the floor, but I hardly took in what was going on. I spent the last ten minutes of his talk in a daze at having spoken to him. I was well chuffed that he'd liked my idea. Loved it, in fact. I couldn't wait to tell Hannah later.

As everyone got up to leave, I noticed Sam making his way over to where I was sitting. I froze to the chair. Ohmigod. He was coming over to speak to me. I could feel myself going red again and breathless as I planned what I'd say. I tried my best to look natural and smile as he approached, but I had a feeling I looked like a grinning hyena, I was so thrilled.

As he reached the front row, he knelt down next to me and turned his back.

"So, did you enjoy the talk?" he asked Nesta.

"Oh, yes," beamed Nesta. "Fascinating."

That wiped the smile off my face. Literally. *Fool*, I thought, you utter *utter* fool. He had no intention of coming to talk to you.

I had a quick look round and prayed that no one had witnessed it, but too late, I noticed Lucy Lovering hovering at the side. She'd seen it all. Me perking up with a stupid grin, then Sam turning his back on me to talk to Nesta. God, how humiliating.

I looked away from Lucy and got up to walk

out the back door. Sam slipped into my vacant chair as though I'd never been there and continued chatting to Nesta.

"Hey, T. J.," called Lucy, as I reached the school gates and turned into the street. "Wait up."

Oh, no. I wanted to get out. Get home and hide. What did she want? I pretended I hadn't heard and carried on walking.

"*T. J.*," said Lucy, catching up.

"Yeah?"

"That was a great answer you gave in there."

"Thanks," I muttered and carried on walking. It didn't feel so great anymore. "Bye, Lucy."

"What bus you getting?" she persisted.

"102."

"Me too. We can go together."

"Aren't you going to wait for Nesta and Izzie?"

"Nah. Izzie's gone off to band practice. And Nesta. Well . . ."

"Probably hoping she'll get a ride from Sam Denham," I said bitterly. I couldn't help it. I felt miffed. Nesta wasn't even interested in writing or going for editor and yet she was the one Sam had

43

picked out for special attention afterward.

"A ride from Sam?" Lucy giggled. "That I'd like to see. He came on a bike."

"Really? I thought he'd come in a flash car or something."

"I know," said Lucy. "But it *is* a flash bike. I saw him arrive on it in a helmet and clips and everything." Then she added, "People aren't always how you think they are."

I felt awkward then and a bit rotten about what I'd thought about Nesta. She can't help being a man magnet.

We stood in silence for a few minutes, then Lucy turned to me. "I hope you don't mind me saying, but . . . back there, I saw . . . you know . . ."

I shrugged and tried to pretend I didn't care. "Well, Nesta *is* gorgeous. She has everything any boy could ever want."

"What? A hairy chest and big muscles?" asked Lucy.

I burst out laughing. "I thought he was coming to talk to me. Or both of us at least."

"I know," said Lucy gently. "I saw."

"I felt a right idiot. Like I was invisible or something."

"I've been there, believe me. I used to feel like that a *lot* when Nesta first arrived," said Lucy. "I mean, I know she's my mate, but she is stunning, so people always look at her before anyone else. And she's funny, so people like her. It's easy to feel left out sometimes. I thought she was going to steal Izzie from me when she first began to hang out with us. I thought she didn't want to be my friend, only Izzie's. It was like I wasn't even there. So, yeah, I know *all* about feeling invisible."

"What did you do?"

"Oh, took a very grown-up approach. Sulked. Acted like a baby. Felt *very* sorry for myself. *Hated* Nesta. Then I got to know her. And discovered that she's really nice. In fact she had been feeling the same way. She thought *I* hated *her* and didn't want to be her friend."

Just at that moment, Sam Denham cycled past on his bike and jolted as he went over a bump in the road.

"If you think about it," said Lucy with a wicked grin, "men really ought to ride sidesaddle."

I burst out laughing as I watched Sam wobble down the road and disappear round a corner.

"And he did call you Lara Croft," said Lucy.

"Yeah, he did, didn't he?" I said. I'd forgotten that. "I thought he meant someone else at first. I guess it's because of my plait."

"Maybe. But you do have a look of her. So, yeah," teased Lucy. "T. J. Watts—invisible? Hardly. Only mistaken for the most sexy woman in cyber-space."

"Yeah," I said. "Don't mess with me. . . ."

I liked Lucy. She was a laugh, like Hannah. She had a way of turning things round and making it all seem okay.

Somehow it didn't seem to matter anymore that Sam Denham had snubbed me. He probably didn't even realize he'd done it.

The rest of the journey home flew by as Lucy and I chatted away. As I let myself into the house later, I realized it was the first time in weeks that I'd actually felt happy.

Things were looking up.

e-mail: Outbox (1)
From: goody2shoes@psnet.co.uk
To: hannahnutter@fastmail.com
Date: 11 June
Subject: Wham Bam thanku Sam

Hi H

Excellent talk by Sam Denham. He fancied Nesta, he made a beeline straight for her after the talk.

I am definitely going to go for editor. Hurrah. And thx for the advice.

Got bus home with Lucy Lovering. She's a real laugh and easy to talk to. She has invited me to her house after school on Friday. Brill. Can't wait.

Scott came over to borrow my *Buffy* vid. He wants to show it to Jessica. He sends his love. He seems to have forgotten he said he'd give me back the money I lent him. I know I should say something, but I can't face it. . . .

Got piles of hwk so better go.

Miss you loads

Spik soon

Love,

T. J.

T. J.

Help. Am mis. Don't like it here. I WANNA come HOME. And now you're going to be best friends with Lucy Lovering and you'll forget me. Started school today. Lots of geeky boys in our class. They have their own language over here. And accent. Like if someone's invited somewhere they say, "Like, yah, rock up when you like man." Or "I rocked up to Jine ee's (Janie's) about farve (five)." And they say "och shame" a lot. And a girlfriend is called a "cherry." It's going to take me ages to learn it all.

    Gudnight ma cherry

    Spik spox spoooon

    Your v sad friend Hannah. Och shame Hannah.

Mark next door has some book titles for you. As he is a boy, they are all rude or stupid.

    Rusty Bedsprings by I. P. Nightly

    Chicken Dishes by Nora Drumstick

    And *The Revelations of St. John* by Armageddin Outtahere

Chapter 5

For Real

"Make yourself at home," said Lucy, flinging her bag down and opening the fridge.

I pulled a chair out at one end of the pine dining table that took up half the kitchen. Before I could sit, I was accosted by a golden Labrador who appeared from under the table. He put his paws up on my chest and began to lick my face with great enthusiasm.

"*Down*, Jerry," said Lucy as another dog appeared next to him and joined in the let's-wash-the-guest's-face game.

"How many are there?" I asked, wiping my face with my sleeve.

"Two," said Lucy, opening the French doors. "Ben! Jerry!" she called as she ran out into the

49

garden. The dogs jumped down and ran after her, tails wagging. Once they were out, Lucy stepped back inside and shut the door. The two dogs looked in through the glass with bemused faces as if to say, "That was a *really* mean trick."

"I didn't mind them," I said. "I like dogs."

"So do I. They're my best friends as much as Iz and Nesta, but they can be a bit much sometimes," said Lucy, then added with a grin, "And so can the dogs."

She held up two cartons of juice. "Cranberry or apple?"

"Cranberry, please," I said, settling into my chair. I liked Lucy's house immediately. It looked like the kind of place you could relax in. "Lived in," as my mum would say. Every surface was covered with books, papers, and magazines, the walls were plastered with paintings and drawings, and there was a lovely old dresser against one wall with colorful bits of mismatched crockery.

"Hi," I said to the boy who was sitting at the other end of the table and reading the latest John Irving novel.

"Uh," he said. Or, at least, that's what it sounded like.

"Steve, this is T. J. T. J., this is my charmer of a brother."

Steve barely looked up. He only grimaced at what his sister had said.

"Oh, hi, T. J.," said Lucy. "I'm Steve. So *pleased* to meet you. I *would* look at you, but then you are my *younger* sister's friend, so why bother? You're too young for me and probably stupid. Nothing you have to say will be of the slightest interest to me. I am your superior in every respect, and everything I say—no, *think*—will be over your head."

Steve's mouth twitched. He almost laughed.

"Good book that," I said, pointing at what he was reading. "I've read all of his, but I liked *The World According to Garp* best."

Then he did look at me. A strange look as though he was considering something unsavory that a cat might have brought in. I met his gaze and tried to look friendly.

"New, are you?" he asked.

"Ohmigod, it speaks," said Lucy, putting a glass of juice beside me. "Sorry about the juice. It's organic, but it tastes okay when you get used to it. My parents are both health freaks, so . . ."

"We have to go out of the house to keep our toxin levels up," said Steve.

"In answer to your question, no, I'm not new," I said. "New here, I guess. But I've been in the same class as Lucy since we began secondary."

"T. J.'s a brainbox like you," said Lucy. "She's going to go for editor of our school newspaper."

"Really," said Steve, looking totally unimpressed.

A brainbox? Was that really how people saw me? How boring.

It got worse.

"She's arm wrestling champion as well," continued Lucy, who was oblivious to the fact that I was squirming in my seat. D'oh. Thanks for the great introduction, Lucy, I thought. Like hi, I'm T. J. Watts, brainbox with muscles. How sexy is that? Not.

Steve put down his book and did what all boys did when my arm wrestling talent was mentioned. He put his hand out.

At that moment, the back door opened and another boy burst in and flung his bag on the table. Blond like Lucy, he looked younger than Steve, maybe fifteen or so, whereas Steve looked like he was in sixth form.

"Excellent," said the boy, plonking himself down next to me. "Arm wrestling. I'll play the winner."

"T. J., other brother, Lal," said Lucy.

We nodded at each other as Steve and I locked hands and put our elbows down. Steve tried to test my strength before we began. I let my hand go limp in his, so he'd think I was weak. This was going to be easy.

"Ready, steady, GO," said Lal.

It was all over in two seconds.

"I wasn't ready," objected Steve, as his lower arm hit the table. "You called GO too soon."

"Rubbish," said Lal, pushing Steve out of his chair and sitting in his place. "You're a puny weakling. Right. Now me."

We locked hands and this time Steve called.

"Ready, steady, GO."

Lal was more of a challenge. Ten seconds.

"Wow. You're pretty good for a girl. Do anything else this well?" he said, picking up my hand and this time stroking it and looking at my mouth with what I can only describe as longing.

Lucy whacked the back of his head. "Take no

notice, T. J. Lal thinks he's Casanova."

Lal dropped my hand and Steve did a kind of smirk. "Don't suppose you can mend computers as well as you arm wrestle, can you?"

"Maybe . . . ," I said.

The rest of the evening went brilliantly.

I fixed Steve's computer no problem. He had one the same make as mine, complete with same operating system. He was well impressed when I pressed a few keys and, hey presto, it worked. He dropped his superior act after that and we got chatting about books. The shelves in his half of the bedroom were heavy with them.

"So who's your favorite author?" he asked.

"God, so many. Can I do top three?"

He nodded.

"Okay, I know that they're kids' books but I still love the Narnia books by C. S. Lewis."

"Yeah. They're cool," he said.

"And I like Bill Bryson."

"Yeah," said Steve, pointing to his shelf. "I've got all of his."

"And I loved *Alias Grace* by Margaret Atwood."

"How's the computer?" called Lucy from the corridor.

"Mended," Steve called back.

"Then stop hogging T. J. She's *my* friend," said Lucy, bursting in the door. "Come and look at my bedroom."

I got up to follow her, feeling well chuffed. She'd called me her friend. I hoped I would be. Steve and Lal, too. They were all really easy to be with and, for once, I hadn't been tongue-tied when meeting boys.

"Wow," I said as Lucy opened the door to her room. "It's like a princess's room. An Indian princess."

"Thanks," said Lucy, looking pleased. "Me and Mum did it last year. The curtain material is from a sari. I got it in the East End."

On one of her walls were cut-outs of people from magazines. Not the usual pop bands and actors—I didn't recognize any of them.

"Who are all these?"

"Dress designers. Gaultier. Armani. Stella McCartney. I want to do design when I leave school."

55

"Well, I can see already that you have a good eye for color, Lucy. This blue, lilac, and silver looks gorgeous. I wish you'd come and do my room. It's so boring. I think the paint Mum used was called Death by Magnolia."

"I'll show you some clothes I've made," said Lucy, opening the wardrobe and pulling out a selection of skirts and tops.

She held some of them up against her and they looked good, even to me, someone who doesn't know a lot about clothes.

"Maybe you could do a fashion piece for my newspaper. Like, what's in for the summer."

"Sort of five top tips?"

"Yeah. Summer sizzlers," I laughed.

"Love to," said Lucy. "And are you going to change the name of the newspaper? *Freemont News* sounds *sooo* boring."

"Exactly what I thought. I *was* going to change it. What do you think of calling it *For Real*?"

"Brilliant," said Lucy, "because that's exactly what it isn't at the moment and it's *exactly* what everyone wants. You're going to be so good at this, T. J. I can tell already that you're going to win."

I shrugged. "I'll give it a go. But I was amazed to find out how many others are going for it after Sam's talk."

"I know," said Lucy. "Even stinky Wendy Roberts, though she was mega-miffed after Sam didn't go for her answer. I saw her face at the back. She was livid. Even more so when he loved yours."

"She's even more angry with me today. She borrowed my math homework and I'd got most of it wrong. Not my fault if it's my worst subject."

"Serves her right," said Lucy as the doorbell rang downstairs. "Don't worry, one of the boys will get it. Probably Nesta, she said she'd come over."

Sure enough, Nesta appeared moments later.

"Hey," she smiled at both of us and flopped on the bed. She looked slightly surprised that I was there, but not unduly bothered. The whole evening was going so well. Maybe I could be friends with her too?

"We were just discussing the newspaper," said Lucy.

"Cool," said Nesta. "So, you going to go for it?"

I nodded. "And Lucy's agreed to do a fashion piece."

"Excellent," said Nesta. "And I tell you what readers like more than *anything*. A makeover. You know, before-and-after sort of thing."

"Good idea," said Lucy.

Nesta was staring at me. "And you know who we should do?"

I shook my head.

"*You,* of course. You could look *fabulous* if you wanted to."

Lucy looked shocked. "Nesta. T. J. *does* look fabulous. Honestly, you and your big mouth. You don't think before you open it, do you?"

"What? *What?*" said Nesta, looking flustered. "I didn't mean anything. . . . I only meant . . ."

I tried to smile but I wanted to die. She thought I looked awful. I knew I didn't wear all the latest fashions, but she didn't have to rub it in. I got up to leave.

"Oh, don't go, T. J.," said Lucy.

I looked at my watch and made for the door. "I have karate at seven and it's the last one before the summer hols, so I can't miss it. Honest, really, it's okay." I did my best to look cheerful, but Lucy didn't look convinced.

"T. J., I hope I didn't . . . ," started Nesta. "Oh, hell. I mean . . . I was only trying to say, I don't think you make . . ."

"Nesta. Button it," said Lucy, linking my arm. "Come on, I'll show you out."

When we got to the front door, Lucy made me promise I'd come again. "You sure you're okay?" she asked.

I nodded. I wanted to get away. And I did have karate that night, not that I was in the mood anymore. I really wanted to go home and talk to Hannah on e-mail.

I looked back at Lucy's house after she shut the front door. No way was I going to go there again for Nesta to point out how awful I look. It's all right for her, she'd look fab in a trash bag.

e-mail: Outbox (2)
From: goody2shoes@psnet.co.uk
To: hannahnutter@fastmail.com
Date: 15 June
Subject: Best friends

To Hannahnutter

I was so wrong about thinking I could be mates with Lucy. Not in a million years. Not while she's friends with Nesta Williams. You won't *believe* what she just said . . . that I need a makeover. So everyone at school pities me. And thinks I'm a swot. And ugly. Everything over here is awful.

I called Scott to ask if he could think of anything I could do to improve my appearance. He laughed and said, you could wear blue more often, it will go with your veins. He thought it was really funny. I said I was upset and needed cheering up and he said he'd phone me back after watching *Friends*. He hasn't phoned back yet.

I miss you loooooaaaaads. Spik spoon.

T. J.

From: goody2shoes@psnet.co.uk
To: hannahnutter@fastmail.com
Date: 15 June
Subject: Where are you?

Hannah. *Where* are you?

Even Scott hasn't phoned me back and he promised.

And Paul will be on the other side of the world now. Probably on some amazing island like in *The Beach*.

I feel so alone.

Love, T. J.

Oh, I met Lucy's bros tonight. They're sweet and the eldest one Steve is okay when he drops his snotty act. He gave me some brill book titles and suggested I put them at the back of the school magazine as a sort of silly fun page.

Bubbles in the Bath by Ivor Windybottom

A Stitch in Time by Justin Case

Chest Pain Remedies by I Coffedalot

Skin Rash Remedies by Ivan Offleitch

WHERE ARE YOU? I have to go to sleep now as it's late.

Chapter 6

Furry Friends

I woke up the next morning feeling better. It was the weekend and Mum had promised to take me to Battersea Dogs' Home. Who needed girl-friends? I was going to get my new best friend of the furry kind.

I got dressed and hurtled down the stairs. Nobody in the kitchen. No one in Dad's study. No one in the living room.

"Where's Mum?" I asked, on finding Dad sitting out on the patio reading the paper and having a cup of coffee.

"She got called out on a case. Good morning, T. J."

"Oh, yeah. Morning. Good. When will she be back?"

"She couldn't say. . . ."

"Oh, *no!*" I wailed. "We were going to go to the

dogs' home. And I have football this after-noon . . . We won't have time if she's not back soon."

"I've got the day off," said Dad. "Ready when you are."

"School all right?" asked Dad, as he drove down Edgware Road toward Hyde Park.

"Yeah."

"Not long until the summer holidays?"

"No. Not long."

"Feeling all right?"

"Yeah. You, Dad?"

"Yes. Fine, thank you."

I could see that he was trying, but I wasn't in the mood for telling him how I was really feeling. He'd never understand how much I missed Paul and Hannah and what it was like to be the only girl in Year Nine without a best friend. Plus, I didn't want to get him started on Paul and how he's wasted his opportunities. The last thing I wanted was a lecture on how I must focus on school and my career and get good grades.

I felt relieved when he gave up and switched the

radio on, even if it was to listen to classical music. He means well, Dad does, but sometimes, he's so busy offering his solutions that he doesn't realize that he hasn't really listened to the problem. It's much easier to talk to Mum. She understands better that sometimes people don't want to be told what to do, they just want someone to listen and give a bit of sympathy.

I spent the rest of the journey looking out of the window as we drove down Park Lane, toward Victoria then over the Chelsea Bridge.

"I've always wanted to come here," said Dad as we parked the car near Battersea Park. "I've been wanting a dog for *ages*."

"Really?" I said as we got out and walked round the corner to the home. "I never knew that. Have you ever had a dog before?"

Dad nodded. "When I was a lad. Best friend I ever had. Being an only child, he was my constant companion."

"What was his name?"

"Rex."

"What happened to him?"

"He died after I left for university. I was heart-broken. I thought it was my fault, you know, because I'd gone away and left him. But my mother said it wasn't like that. She said it was his time to go and that he'd waited until I'd gone so as not to upset me."

We walked into the reception area at the home and I watched Dad as he found his wallet to pay our entrance fee. I swear his eyes misted over when he'd talked about Rex. It made me see him in a new light. Dad clearly had a soft side when it came to animals.

"Pound for you," said the lady behind a counter. "And fifty pence for the young lady. Have you come to look or to buy a dog or cat?"

"Buy a dog," I said.

"Then you need to have an interview with a Rehomer first. Follow the red paws on the ground and someone will come and talk to you. See what sort you want and so on. Then you follow the blue paws and go and have a look."

I couldn't wait and felt really excited. I could see Dad did as well. He'd turned from Scary Dad into Smiley Dad.

We followed the red paws and went to sit in the waiting room with a group of other people. A sign on the wall told us that it cost £70 for a dog and £40 for a cat. After a short wait, a man in a red tracksuit came out and called us into a room where he asked loads of questions about where we lived and whether there were other children or cats and if was there a garden.

It was funny because he was stern like a headmaster and Dad had to really sell the fact that we would be good owners.

"Our chief concern," said the man, finally relaxing, "is that the dogs go to a permanent home where they will be happy and well cared for—for the rest of their lives. Hence the interrogation. Many of our dogs are here because their previous owners couldn't or wouldn't care for them. Last thing we want is for a dog to have another bad experience."

"Quite right," said Dad. "I can assure you that we'll take very good care of whomever we get today."

"Okay, then. Let's go and look at the dogs," said the man.

Dad looked at me and winked as we followed the man along the path of blue paws through a courtyard to a building at the back.

Inside it was like a hospital with long sloping corridors leading up to different floors. Each corridor had a different name: Oxford Street on the ground floor where the clinic was; Bond Street and Bow Street on the first floor where the dogs were kept; Regent Street and Baker Street on the second with dogs and cats and a private floor, Fleet Street and Pall Mall on the top.

"Here we go," said our Rehomer, opening a door to a side ward. "I'll leave you to look around. Take your time, then, when you've decided, we'll bring the dog to you for an introduction and see if you get on. Takes about fifteen minutes. Then, if all parties are happy, you can go."

Two things hit us as soon as we entered the ward. The sound of barking. And the smell. Not a bad smell, but distinctive nonetheless. Like wet hay mixed with dog food.

"Phworr," I said.

"Aromatherapy of the canine kind," laughed

Dad as we looked in to see the first hopeful face looking out at us from behind bars.

"It's like they're in a prison cell," I said as a Jack Russell poked a paw through at us and barked in friendly greeting.

We spent the next hour walking through all the ward on every floor. We must have seen about fifty dogs. Each one had a little room in which was a blanket, water, a toy, and outside access to a corridor at the back.

There were all sorts of characters to choose from. Collies, beagles, Jack Russells, muts of every color, even a Samoyed, which Dad told me was a rare breed. He looked like a big white teddy. At the side of each cage was a report with the dog's details: the breed, name, age, history, and whether they liked cats or children. Whether they needed an experienced owner and whether they were destructive or not!

At the end of their report was a comment as though written by the dog. "I make a good companion." Or "I need commitment." Or one big dog whose comment said, "I am a majestic individual!"

"That one sounds like you, Dad," I said, pointing at the last one. With his tall stature and silver-white hair, Dad did have a majestic air.

"I don't know what you mean," he laughed, then pointed at one that said, "And there's one that sounds like you: 'I have a strong will and need a lot of training.'"

On one ward, a black mut called Woodie was doing everything he could to get people's attention. All sorts of mad antics—bouncing off the walls, paws up against the bars. It was as though he was saying "pick me, *pick me*, look what I can *do* . . . back flips, jumping, bouncing!!!! Pick me. *Pick me.*"

Another old brown-and-white collie sat looking at us with pleading eyes. She looked as though she had a bad wig on.

"This is heartbreaking," said Dad, reading her report. "She's called Kiki. She's thirteen."

Kiki put her paw through the cage and even though there was a big sign saying not to touch the dogs, Dad took her paw and stroked it. "Hello, girl." Then he turned to me and I swear his eyes were misting over again. "Poor thing. At her age, she's probably here because her owner died or something. She looks as though she's been well looked after though. Shame, because a lot of people come here and only want the young dogs. They see 'thirteen years' and see the expense of vet's bills."

I was finding it excruciatingly difficult. I wanted all of them. Every ward we went into, the dogs would perk up and start wagging their tails as though Dad and I were their best and oldest friends. So pleased to see us. It was like they were saying, "Oh *there* you are, hold on a mo, I'll just get my stuff and we can go." Then, as we walked past their cages, their faces would fall and their tails would go down as if thinking, "Come back. Hey, where are you going? I thought we were outta here?"

"Can't we hire a coach, Dad, and come back with it and say right, everyone in? And then go and buy a big house in the country . . ."

"I wish," said Dad. "But, sadly, we can only have one. Have you made up your mind?"

I shook my head. I'd fallen in love with about six of them. Woodie and the Samoyed and Kiki the old collie, a mut that looked like an old teddy, a beautiful black Alsatian, and a cheeky Jack Russell.

Some had to be overlooked as it said clearly on their report that they could be destructive and didn't like children, even teens. Others, I knew, were too big, like the Alsatian. Arm wrestling champion that I am, I knew I wouldn't be able to keep him on a lead.

It was then that I turned a corner and saw Mojo. He was sitting quietly in his room, a medium-size black dog with a white patch over one eye. He gazed up at us with the saddest eyes I've ever seen. You look how I felt last night, I thought. Sad, lonely, and badly in need of a friend. "Mojo is four years old and a stray," said his report. "He has a very gentle nature and likes people. He is very distressed at finding himself here and would like a good home as soon as possible."

Mojo looked up at me with hopeful eyes.

I glanced over at Dad.

"He's The One, isn't he?" said Dad.

I nodded.

Dad and I didn't stop talking all the way home. He told me all about how he had wanted to be a vet, but didn't think he could cope with having to put people's pets down as you sometimes had to do.

We even talked about Paul.

"At least this fella won't get on a plane and leave us," said Dad, looking at Mojo, who was sitting happily in the back, looking out the window. "Unlike some people I could mention."

"Paul, you mean?"

Dad nodded. "I hope he's all right, wherever he's got to. He may be grown-up, but you never stop worrying. And I know you and Mum think I go on, but I know my own son and he can be naive at the best of times. Even as a young lad, he was a dreamer, too trusting of people. . . . You have to have your wits about you when you're traveling."

"He'll be okay," I said. "He's with Saskia."

"Hmmmph," said Dad. "And she's as daft as he is. Still, I guess he's not alone. You're right."

I was glad it had been Dad who'd come with me to the home. I felt I'd got to know him better. And discovered he was missing Paul as much as I was.

When we got home, Mojo ran around sniffing everything. Tail wagging happily, he seemed more than pleased when Dad opened the French doors to the garden. He ran out and sniffed the air as if he couldn't get enough of it.

"I think he likes it here," said Mum, watching him from the kitchen. As he ran about familiarizing himself with the smells, the phone rang.

"Oh, that will be someone called Lucy again. She's phoned a few times since I've been back and so has someone called Nesta."

I went to answer the call. Mum was right. It was Lucy.

"About Nesta last night," she said. "She really didn't mean to upset you. What she meant to say was that with your potential you could look totally amazing. She wasn't saying you looked awful or anything."

I'd forgotten all about the incident the night before. And it didn't seem so bad in the light of a new day.

"I suppose I *was* being a bit oversensitive," I admitted. "Overreacted a bit."

"We all have days like that," said Lucy. "Like my mum says, only the wearer of the shoe knows where it rubs. You know, sometimes we don't know where each other's sensitive spots are and tread on them by mistake. Nesta treads on people's sensitive spots with hobnailed boots on. But she doesn't mean to. We all want to be friends. Honest. We all agreed. That's why Nesta came to sit next to you at Sam's talk the other afternoon."

"Really? I thought that was just coincidence."

"No. It was so you had someone to sit with."

"Really?"

We chatted on for about ten minutes and I told her my news about Mojo. She wants to come over on Monday to meet him.

After I put the phone down, I had plenty to think about. It looked like I had misjudged the whole situation and I decided I should give Nesta another chance. I watched Mojo as he ran about. He looked a different dog already. His tail was wagging madly, his tongue out.

Mum had her radio on in the kitchen and an old song was blasting out. How true, I thought, as I listened to the lyrics. "What a difference a day makes, twenty-four little hours . . ."

We're all going to be good friends, I thought, going out into the garden to Mojo and doing what

I'd wanted to do ever since I'd set eyes on him.

I gave him a big hug.

---

e-mail:	Inbox (1)
From:	hannahnutter@fastmail.com
To:	goody2shoes@psnet.co.uk
Date:	16 June
Subject:	Asta la vista

Ola bamboo baby.
Me velly sollee no e-mail back last night.

Sollee you had bad time. Wish I was there to make it all better. Confucius, he say all things will pass. Particularly if you eat plennee fiber. Arf, arf.

Had brill time. Went for a grand beano feast and drinky drunky woos at a girl from school's. She's new like me only she's come here from Johannesburg (known over here as Jo'burg). I think we might be friends. Her name's Rachel.

Am getting bronzed and beautiful. It may be okay here after all.

She has two book titles for you. Bit rude.
Poo on the Wall by Hoo Flung Dung
Dog Bites by R. Stornaway
Love you loads,
Hannah

e-mail: Outbox (1)
From: goody2shoes@psnet.com
To: hannahnutter@fastmail.com
Date: 16 June
Subject: Illo mysterio of lifeio

Great to hear from you. All changed from last night. V happy. Have new furry friend called Mojo. He's adorable and Mum says he can sleep in my room. I think Dad is jealous. He was so sweet today at the dogs' home. I realized I don't know my dad as well as I thought. He's v worried because Paul said he'd call when he got to Goa but nothing so far. Hope he's okay. I think it's just Paul and he'll call when he remembers.

Also, Lucy called and apologized about Nesta. May be okay after all, but no one will ever replace you. I am glad you met this new girl though as I don't want you to be lonely. Lucy said her bro Steve liked me and thought it was unusual to meet a girl who had half a brain and was good to talk to. Not sure if this is a good thing as boys seem to view me as "one of the lads" and I would like to have a boyfriend some day. Maybe Nesta was right. Maybe I do need a makeover. Anyway, I told Mum I want to change my appearance and maybe try and look a bit more like a girl. She was v pleased and said I can have a new dress.

Scott came over to meet Mojo. He has ditched Jessica already. He was looking mucho cute and was very sweet with Mojo.

Funny business, life, isn't it? Just when you think everything's rotten and life stinks, it can all change. Love you.

T. J.

Books:
Rhythm of the Night by Mark Time
Bad Falls by Eileen Dover

---

e-mail: Inbox (1)
From: paulwatts@worldnet.com
To: goody2shoes@psnet.co.uk
Date: 17 June
Subject: Goa

Hey T. J.

In Goa, it's awesome. We sleep under the stars and look out over the sea. We met some amazing people (travelers mostly—Brits and Irish and a large number of Dutchies) and the locals here are very kind. I have bought an amazing crystal, and every time I hold it, it is like there are enormous beams of light pulsating through my head via my temples, brow and crown chakra, but it gives Saskia a headache. I have been having real funky lucid dreams lately and been feeling like a million dollars with this quartz.

Rock on.

Paul

P.S. Please let Ma and Pa know I am okay. Tried to ring but lost wallet soon after we arrived. Have got job in a bar though. So all okay. Please ask Ma to send some dosh. Tell her I'll pay her back, promise, promise. Don't mention to Dad. Saskia got some nasty insect bites. Please ask Ma to send some more homeopathic stuff—arnica and apis and citronella and lavender oil.

Chapter 7

Dog
of the Week

Our class was in a mad mood the next week at school. I think the heat wave had affected everyone's brain.

It started in science, when Mr. Dixon asked if anyone knew the formula for water.

Gabby Jones put her hand up. "HIJKLMNO," she said proudly.

"Er, can you tell me why?" he asked.

"Yesterday, sir," said Gabby, "you said H to O was the formula for water."

"H *two* O." He sighed, then wrote on the board. "H two, as in the *number*, O. Okay, last question about water. What can we do to save water in a water shortage?"

"Put less in the kettle, sir," said Lucy.

"Excellent. Anyone else?"

"Don't use the hose," I said.

"Another good one. Any others to help our water supply go further?"

Jade Wilcocks' hand shot up. "Dilute it, sir," she said.

Mr. Dixon shook his head, but I could see he was trying not to laugh.

Then it was into the school hall for a film about the cosmos and all the planets and stars. Afterward, Miss Watkins asked us questions to see if we'd been paying attention, as I think some girls used the hour in the dark as an excuse to have a kip.

"What is a comet?" asked Miss Watkins.

I knew the answer to this and put my hand up.

"Star with a tail, miss."

"Correct. And can anyone name one?"

Candice Carter, who was one of those I saw nodding off, stuck her hand up. "Mickey Mouse, miss," she said as everyone cracked up.

★ ★ ★

But the best was in R.E. Again, it was poor Miss Watkins taking the class and she asked if anyone knew what God's name was.

This time it was Mo Harrison who put her hand up.

"Andy, miss."

"Andy? Why on earth would Andy be the name of God?"

"It's in all the hymns, miss," said Mo. "Andy walks with me. Andy talks with me . . . There are loads of examples."

"No, Mo," Miss Watkins said, turning to Nesta who was crying with laughter. "Nesta Williams, seeing as you clearly find it so funny. What do *you* think the name of God might be?"

"Er, not sure," said Nesta, looking caught out. "What do you think?"

"I don't think," said Miss Watkins. "I *know*."

"I don't think I know either," giggled Nesta.

The whole class got detention, but it was worth it. I felt like I'd spent the whole morning laughing my head off.

We never did get to know what God's name was.

★ ★ ★

"How are you getting on with the mag?" asked Izzie as we sat doing our lines in detention in the lunch break.

"So-so. I've got some ideas, but need to get them down on paper," I replied.

"Come over to ours at the weekend," said Lucy. "I'm sure Steve would like to see you again, and he can help. And so could me and Izzie and Nesta."

The offer of help was tempting. Less than two weeks to go until the entries were due in and there was going to be a lot of competition. Intense discussions and hushed conversations were going on everywhere.

"I could do a horoscope page for you, if you like," said Izzie.

"That would be brilliant," I said. "And I may do a piece about Battersea Dogs' Home."

I showed Lucy and Izzie the Polaroids of Mojo. Soon, everyone wanted to look, so they got passed round the class. Everyone ooed and aahed until it got to Wendy Roberts.

"Arrr, *sweet,*" she said loudly. "T. J.'s new boyfriend. Hey, T. J. Is this *all* you can pull? He needs a bit of a shave."

A few girls giggled half-heartedly, but as though they felt they had to rather than because they thought Wendy was hilarious. Why was she being so horrid to me? Was it because Sam had liked my answer and not hers? Or because she'd got a low mark after copying my homework? It wasn't my fault I was crapola at math. I racked my brains for something funny to say back so it would look like I didn't care, but I couldn't think of anything quick enough. Bummer and bananas, as Hannah used to say. Why can I never come up with the right words when I need them?

After detention, we all trooped out to the playground for the last ten minutes of lunch. I ate my sandwiches and stretched out in the sun, but I couldn't help but notice that some girls were passing a piece of paper round, then staring at me and giggling in a nervous way.

Oh, what now? I thought as Izzie came out to join me on the bench.

"What's going on?" I asked.

"Oh, Wendy. You know she's running for editor as well. She's just jealous. . . ."

"Take no notice," said Lucy, coming to join us.

"You don't need to know, T. J. She's a sad cow and you should ignore her."

"No, I want to see," I said, and got up and went over to a group of girls who were standing round Wendy looking at the piece of paper. I glanced over Wendy's shoulder. There was a picture of a dog with its head cut out and mine stuck on instead. She'd cut out the photo of me from the group shot in last month's newspaper. Underneath Wendy had written "Dog of the Week."

"What do you think, T. J.?" giggled Wendy. "You getting your dog gave me the idea. Each month in the newspaper, we pick someone to be Dog of the Week. What do you think?"

As I searched for the right put-down, a voice behind me got in first. "I think, Wendy, that if you were any more stupid, you'd have to be watered."

I turned round and there was Nesta. She looked mad.

She took the paper and, much to Wendy's astonishment, she ripped it up. "This is not remotely funny, Wendy. And you know it's not. It's not journalism. It's just nastiness. Come on, T. J. Don't lower yourself by breathing the same air as this lowlife."

I was as gobsmacked as Wendy, but I turned away with Nesta and followed her to a bench where Lucy and Izzie were sitting.

"Thanks, Nesta," I said, "but I was okay. I can handle Wendy Roberts."

"I know. But I've been waiting for a chance to show you that I'm on your side. I'm sorry about the other day. Sometimes words come out the wrong way."

"Not just then," I grinned. "That was brilliant. I wish I could come out with stuff like that. I always think of good things to say later, like when I'm falling asleep or something. . . ."

"Nesta's special talent is fighting for her mates," teased Lucy. "Her special downfall is her big gob."

"Well, I know what it's like to have some saddo like Wendy have it in for you," said Nesta.

"I don't know why. I never did anything to her."

"With her sort you don't have to," said Nesta. "She's probably jealous."

"Of me? Don't be mad."

"Looks and brains," said Nesta. "Lethal combination."

I felt really chuffed. Maybe she didn't think I looked too bad after all.

Then I looked over at Wendy who was glowering at us from the other side of the playground. I hoped this wasn't going to be the start of something.

Then I looked at Lucy, Izzie, and Nesta glowering back at her like they were my best mates. And I hoped that this *was* going to be the start of something.

---

e-mail: Outbox (1)
From: goody2shoes@psnet.co.uk
To: hannahnutter@fastmail.com
Date: 18 June
Subject: notalot

Dear H

Weather is lovely. Wish you were here.

T. J.

```
e-mail:      Inbox (2)
From:        hannahnutter@fastmail.com
To:          goody2shoes@psnet.co.uk
Date:        18 June
Subject:     notalot either
```

Dear T. J.

Weather is here. Wish you were lovely. Arf arf.
Must dash. Going to movie, i.e., Drive-in.
Bigola hugs and heeheehasta la vista baby.
Hannah

Book title:
Chest Complaints by Ivor Tickliecoff

```
From:        nestahotbabe@retro.co.uk
To:          goody2shoes@psnet.co.uk
Date:        18 June
Subject:     Friday night
```

Hey, Lara Croft
Wanna come to a sleepover Friday night? Iz and
Lucy are coming. About 7?
Nesta

Chapter 8

Sleepover Secrets

"T. J. T. J.!" called Mum excitedly as she came in the door. "Where are you?"

"Here," I called from upstairs, where I was straining to get started on some ideas for the school magazine. So far, I'd written one word. Aggh.

It was Friday night and I was going to the sleepover at Nesta's in half an hour. An evening of culture had been planned. *The Simpsons* and *Buffy* on Sky, then *EastEnders*, *Friends*, and *South Park*.

Mum came in carrying a large carrier bag and plonked herself on the bed. She looked *very* pleased with herself.

"I couldn't resist," she said, getting something wrapped in tissue out of the bag. She pulled out a calf-length dress with swirly rust, maroon, and orange-colored flowers on it.

"What do you think?" she asked.

The word *disgusting* came to mind, though I suppose it was pretty in that cottage-chintzy-curtain-fabric way.

"Not your *usual* taste, Mum," I said, thinking I was being diplomatic. Mum isn't fashion-conscious at the best of times, but her style is more plain than flowery. Jaeger and Country Casuals for work and sloppy tracksuits for the weekend. And her idea of making an effort to dress up is to wear a blue glass bead necklace. Even if it's with the tracksuit.

"Not for me, silly," said Mum. "It's for *you*."

Whaaat? Aggggh. No. *Buuuut it's horrid*, I thought.

"It's lovely, isn't it? I saw it in a little boutique opposite the surgery and remembered what you'd said about wanting to look more like a girl. Perfect, I thought. I described you to the lady in the shop, said you had dark hair and hazel eyes and she said you'd be an Autumn according to her Color Me Beautiful chart and would suit the brown rusty colors," said Mum, not drawing breath. "Cost a fortune but we won't tell Dad. It's about time you had something nice. So what do you think?"

She was so delighted with her purchase that I didn't have the heart to hurt her feelings.

"There aren't words," I said truthfully.

"I *knew* you'd love it. You can wear it to your new friend's house, can't you? Try it on, try it on."

I smiled weakly as I desperately searched for something to say. Hmm? *How* do I get out of this one?

Ten minutes later, I was in the kitchen wearing the dress and still wondering, literally, how to get out of this. Course, that had to be the very moment Scott banged on the back door.

"Evenin' all," he said, letting himself in and stroking Mojo, who jumped up in greeting. Then he saw me. "Yuk. You going to a fancy dress?"

"Shhh," I said. "Mum's upstairs. She bought it for me."

"What, to wear?"

"No. To scare off burglars. *Yes*, to wear."

Scott pulled a face. "You look weird. Like you're in *The Waltons*."

"Thanks a bunch. So how do I get out of it?"

Scott went round to my back, put his hands on my waist and nuzzled into my neck. "Now *that's* one thing I'm good at, helping girls out of their dresses." He started to stroke my hair then play with my zip. "Now, Miss Watts," he whispered. "I really don't think this is your style. Let me help you out of it and into something . . . more . . . comfortable."

I giggled and slapped him, hoping he didn't see me blushing. Him nibbling my neck made me feel all fluttery inside. Nice.

"Uhyuh yunnawee," I started to say, then took a deep breath and made myself remember this was Scott *for heaven's sake*. "Seriously though," I said, turning so he couldn't see my red face. "I'm going to a sleepover tonight at a new mate's house and I can't possibly wear this. She'll think it's so naff."

"What new mate?"

"Oh," I suddenly remembered he fancied Nesta. "Er . . . Nesta Williams new mate."

"You're kidding. *Nesta?* Why didn't you tell me? When did this all happen? I thought you said she was an airhead."

"Well, I was wrong. She's actually very nice."

Scott punched the air. "*Yes*. Will you promise, promise, *promise* to put a word in for me? Or even better, you could bring her here and I could kind of casually drop in and you could introduce us?"

I *could* I suppose, I thought, watching Scott as he went into the hall and checked himself in the mirror. I just wish that a boy would feel that enthusiastic about me one day. And even more to my surprise, I found myself thinking, I wish *Scott* would feel that enthusiastic about me.

By the time I was due to go, I had a plan.

I went down into the kitchen wearing my usual tracksuit and trainers to find Mum chopping peppers and onions on the counter.

"I can't wear the dress tonight, Mum. I'm going via Lucy's house and they've got two huge dogs. Labradors. *Very* hairy. *Always* moulting. The kind of dogs who jump up on you. With *enormous* claws and muddy paws and they like to chew everything. They'd *ruin* my dress. Do you mind if I put it away for a special occasion?" (Special occasion like Bonfire Night and I put it on a guy to be burned, I thought.)

"Sure," said Mum. "And are you *sure* you like it?"

Was she giving me a get out? I was about to open my mouth and say *nooooo*, I hate it . . .

"Because they had it in pink," she said.

Ag. Agh. Agherama.

Later, I thought, as I made for the door. I will sort this later.

"Got your jimjams?" asked Nesta, closing the front door behind us. She looked fab in a lilac cami set with the words *Groovy Chick* across the top.

I nodded as she led me through into a living room with high ceilings, deep-red walls, and plush brown velvet sofas. Impressive, I thought, as I took in the mix of dark wood and Turkish and Moroccan-looking rugs.

Izzie and Lucy were already there, curled up for our telly night, and both gave me a wave. Izzie was wearing red flannel pajamas with fluffy sheep on them, and Lucy had blue ones with stars and moons all over. I waved back and hoped that they couldn't see how nervous I was feeling. Nesta's flat was so glam, I hoped they wouldn't think my house was mega-dull when they came to visit me.

"You can change in there," said Nesta, showing me a cloakroom off the hall. "No one's here. Tony's staying over at a mate's, and Mum and Dad have gone out to eat. Mum said we can order pizza. What's your fave?"

"Four cheese. Please," I said as I closed the cloakroom door behind me.

"Coming up," called Nesta. *"Quattro formaggi."*

My pajamas looked so boring as I got them out of my bag. A pale grey vestie thing for the top and bottoms to match. Ah well. What you see is what you get, I thought, as I pulled them on, then went back into the living room and pulled a cushion onto the floor.

"Let the viewing commence," said Izzie, passing me the Pringles.

After we'd finished watching *South Park* and munching our way through crisps, pizza, chocolate, and ice cream, the real fun began. Nesta put on a *Riverdance* video. After we'd danced our socks off for fifteen minutes, we all collapsed on the sofa and they talked about *everything*—music, clothes, mags, school gossip, horoscopes, and, finally, boys.

As they chatted, we painted each other's toenails. I did Nesta's dark purple and then she did mine the same color. Izzie did Lucy's pale blue and she did Iz's red. None of them seemed to mind that I didn't say a lot. I was happy to sit back and take it all in.

Nesta was a hoot and seemed to be *very* experienced with boys. She's had loads of boyfriends. At least eight. Maybe more, I lost count. And she seems to be an expert on snogging.

Izzie is just fab. She's into loads of interesting stuff, not just horoscopes but alternative health, food, nutrition, aromatherapy, crystals, and witchcraft. And she's *also* in a band with her boyfriend. His name's Ben and the band's called King Noz. She sang a song for us that she'd written herself. She has the most amazing voice.

And Lucy. Lucy's sweet. And kind. She kept checking on me to see I had enough to drink and eat. And was I comfortable. Did I need another cushion?

They all made me feel so welcome I suppose it was inevitable that, in the end, they'd turn the spotlight on me.

"So T. J., is there anyone you fancy?"

I shook my head. "Not really."

"So why've you gone red?" asked Nesta.

"Nesta!" said Lucy.

"What? *What?*"

"Let her tell in her own time," said Izzie.

I decided to plunge in. They'd all been so open with me, I felt I should be the same with them.

"Well, I suppose there *is* one boy," I said. "I've known him all my life, but he treats me more like one of the lads than a girl."

"Does he know you fancy him?" asked Lucy.

"*Noooo*. In fact," I said, looking at Nesta, "he fancies you."

"*Me?*"

"Yeah, he's seen you at the Hollywood Bowl and asked if I'd put a word in."

Nesta looked surprised. "What's his name?"

"Scott Harris."

"Don't know him," said Nesta. "And anyway, I have a boyfriend."

"Posh boy," teased Lucy.

"Simon Peddington Lee," said Izzie in a voice like the Queen's.

"He's away at school at the mo," said Nesta, "but we speak or text most days. He'll be back soon for the summer hols. And, *anyway*, I don't steal other girl's boyfriends."

"He's not my boyfriend."

"Not *yet*," said Nesta. "Anyway, you saw him first ,so in my book that means he's yours whether he knows it or not."

"Maybe you should let him know you like him," said Iz.

"*Noooo*. Can't. *No*. You don't understand. That would ruin everything. See, he's one of the few boys I can talk to. I have known him so long I don't get all tongue-tied like I do around boys I fancy."

"You got on with my brothers okay," said Lucy.

"Yeah. But that was different."

"Ah, you don't fancy Steve. Is that it?"

"No. Yes. I don't know. I didn't think about it. It felt so natural round your house, I kind of forgot he was a boy. And, well . . . it's just, we got off on the right foot. I won at arm wrestling and we were away."

"Got off on the right arm then," grinned Lucy. "Not foot."

I decided to tell them everything. "See, I can karate-chop a boy to the floor and stand on his neck easy peasy, but the thought of having to kiss one and I'm terrified."

"Ah . . . ," said Lucy. "I get it."

"You have to be like Buffy," said Izzie. "Like, one minute she's snogging Angel, the next, she's out vaporizing vampires. It's a question of balance."

"Right," I said, feeling more confused than ever.

I could see Nesta was bursting to say something.

"What?" I said.

"Nothing," she said, but she was holding her stomach as though keeping something in.

"Spill. I can take it."

"No. Nothing. Well. What if . . . ? No . . . nothing . . ."

"Oh, for God's sake, Nesta. Spit it out," said Izzie.

"Well," said Nesta. "How about you don't tell

Scott you fancy him? How about we get him to fancy *you*?"

"Ah," I said. "And how do you propose to do that?"

I knew exactly what she had in mind, but felt like teasing her.

"Er . . . ," she looked anxiously at Lucy. "Dunno really."

I decided to help her out. "You still want to do a makeover, don't you?"

"Er, *no*," she said with a quick glance at Lucy.

"You think I look like a bag lady, don't you?"

"*NO*. I never said *that*!" Now Nesta looked really worried. Lucy may be small in height but she's clearly big in Nesta's books. "No. *No*. I think you look fab. Oh, all right. . . . I think you could look fabber. With a makeover. That's all. And now you're going to hate me. And think I'm mean because I want to help. And Lucy's going to go on about my big gob. And how I never know when to stop. . . ."

I laughed. "I'm only teasing you. No, please, do it. To tell the truth, I took a look at myself in the mirror this evening in the dress from hell that my mum bought me and I thought, T. J., you need help. I'd love it if you gave me a makeover. I'll use it in the magazine. And . . . anyone got a pen? I've had an idea for a feature for the mag. A Sleepover Special Report."

Nesta handed me a pen and paper from the drawer in the desk behind the sofa. Then she took my face in her hands and turned it to profile and back. Then she clapped her hands and went into drama luvvie persona, "A mi-vake over. Oh, *daaahlling*, ve're going to mi-vake you look *faaaabulouse.*"

D'oh, I thought. What've I let myself in for?

Sleepover Special Report

Ever wondered what makes the perfect sleepover? *For Real* asked four teenagers for their top tips and fave ingredients. Here's what they came up with.

Five main ingredients
1) Nosh for the munchies
2) Drinks

---

3) Videos
4) Music
5) Makeup for makeovers
6) Mags

Special Spot Report

Izzie Foster. 14. Aquarius. Finchley. London
Fave thing to do at sleepovers? Goss. Listen to music.
Nosh.
Fave music for sleepover? Anastacia. Christina
Aguilera.
Fave video? *Austin Powers 2.* Yeah baby yeah.
Top nosh? Choc-chip cookies. Doritos.
Top drink? Organic elderflower juice.

Nesta Williams. 14. Leo. Highgate. London
Fave thing to do at sleepovers? Dance. Read problem
page in mags and have a good laugh. Makeovers.
Fave music for sleepover? Destiny's Child. Craig David.
Fave video? *Charlie's Angels* or *Scream.*
Top nosh? Nettuno pizza with extra cheese. Häagen
Dazs.
Top drink? Coke.

Lucy Lovering. 14. Gemini. Muswell Hill. London

Fave thing to do at sleepovers? Talk about snogging and boys.

Fave music for sleepover? Robbieeee.

Fave video? *Titanic*. I'm King of the Wooooorld.

Top nosh? Chinese take-away. Yum. Pecan nut Häagen Dazs.

Top drink? Hot chocolate made with milk and marshmallows.

T. J. Watts. 14. Sagittarius. Muswell Hill. London

Fave thing to do at sleepovers? Chill. Laugh my head off.

Fave music for sleepover? *Top of the Pops* summer CD.

Fave video? *South Park Christmas Special* starring Mr. Stinky the Christmas Poo.

Top nosh? Burger and chips. Toffee popcorn.

Top drink? Banana milk shake with vanilla ice cream on top.

Chapter 9

American Pie

"So The Plan is," said Nesta, through a mouthful of toast, "we all go to T. J.'s and sift through her wardrobe."

It was Saturday morning and we were still in our jimjams, sitting round in the kitchen, eating toast, and drinking milky coffees.

I wondered if I could get out of The Plan. Not that I was bothered about the makeover anymore, no, I was worried what the girls were going to make of the Wrinklies. Izzie, Lucy, and Nesta's parents were normal ages. And Nesta's are so *glamorous*. I met them this morning while I was waiting for the bathroom. Her mum's a newsreader on cable television and her dad's a film director and both *très* good looking and stylish as far as grown-ups go.

Mainly though, I was worried what the Wrinklies might make of the girls. Dad in particular. He can turn into Scary Dad at the slightest bit of noise or disturbance. Our house was never one to throw its doors open and welcome in the neighborhood. I always used go to Hannah's house rather than the other way round. Dad likes his privacy, the fewer people he sees when he's not working, the better. Radio 4 and peace and quiet and he's happy. Last thing I wanted was him showing me up in front of new friends by asking them pointed questions like, "What time's your bus home?"

I thought I'd better warn the girls.

"Okay, er, about my parents, well my dad . . . ," I said, and explained the situation.

"Same at our house," said Izzie. "My mum doesn't exactly encourage me to bring my mates back. Some parents are like that. It's easy to hang at Lucy's or here where no one's running round cleaning up after you all the time."

"So, no problemo, T.J.," said Nesta. "We will be the perfect example of quiet refined teenagers."

"Well behaved and demure," said Izzie.

"And *very* mature," said Lucy.

I breathed a sigh of relief. I could trust them to be cool. At that moment, the back door opened and Leonardo DiCaprio's younger Italian brother walked in. I mean, this boy was *seriously* handsome.

"T. J., Tony. Tony, T. J. My brother," said Nesta as if I hadn't realized.

"Hi, T.J.," said The Vision.

"Hi, Tony," said a friendly voice inside my head. However, what came out of my mouth was, *"uhyuh."* Oh, *noooo*, I thought. Alien Girl from the Planet Zog is back to haunt me.

Tony looked at the croissant I was about to eat, then looked right into my eyes and did a half-smile that made him look even more gorgeous. "So, T. J., what do virgins eat for breakfast?"

"Dunno," I replied, breaking his gaze and staring at the floor.

"Thought so," he said and laughed.

"Take no notice of Tony, he's a dingbat," said Nesta. "So. Aren't you going to ask?"

"Ask what?"

"How come Tony is my brother?"

"No."

"Why not?" asked Nesta. "*Everyone* asks. He's light-skinned, I'm dark-skinned, how come?"

"Obvious," I said. "Same father, different mothers."

"Hmmm," said Nesta. "Smart cookie."

Not really, the voice in my head said. I met your mum and dad this morning. I know she's Jamaican and your dad looks Italian. Tony looks like your dad so I reckon he must have had a different mother. Elementary, my dear Williams. However, Noola the Alien Girl is a person of few words and all that came out was, "*uh.*" Smart cookie indeed. Why did this *always* happen when boys I fancied were around?

"My real mum died before I knew her. I was six months old," explained Tony, coming over and laying his head on my shoulder. "Really, I'm an orphan. An orphan prince who needs *love* and *affection*."

"*Uhyuh,*" I stuttered, hoping that by some strange quirk of fate, Tony might be fluent in Zoganese.

I could see Lucy giving me a strange look then giving Tony a *filthy* look. Hmm? Something going on there, methinks. Must ask later.

Tony went over to the fridge and opened the door. "What's to eat?" He got out a half-eaten apple pie, put it on the breakfast bar, and cut himself a huge slice.

"Apple pie for breakfast?" said Iz. "Ew. Gross."

He turned and grinned at her. "Would you prefer I did something else with it?"

"Like what?" said Iz.

"You seen that film *American Pie*?"

"Yeah," said Izzie, then pulled a face. "*Ew*, double gross."

"What are you on about?" I asked.

Nesta looked at Tony wearily and sighed. "Sorry about my disgusting brother, T. J. In *American Pie*, a boy asks what it's like to have sex. His mate says it's like putting your thingee in a warm apple pie."

I blushed furiously as Tony watched me closely to see my reaction.

"Apparently some guy in Australia tried it," said Lucy, getting down from her stool at the breakfast bar and refilling the kettle. "Steve read about it in the paper. This guy didn't wait for the pie to cool when it came out of the oven. He was taken to the local hospital and treated for burns."

"*Aggghhh,*" said Tony, putting his hands over his crotch as the rest of us laughed. "I wonder how he explained *that* to the nurse on duty."

Lucy looked at the apple pie and I saw a wicked twinkle appear in her eye. "Would you like me to warm that up for you, Tony?" she asked sweetly. "I could put it in the microwave. On high?"

Tony went over to her and put his arm round her. "And how *is* the love of my life?"

"Dunno. How is she?" said Lucy as she took his arm away from her shoulder.

"You know you want me really," said Tony.

Lucy began to walk out of the kitchen. "Yeah. Right. It's *agony* keeping my hands off you. Not."

"That girl . . ." Tony sighed as he watched her go out of the room. "So what are you lot doing today?"

"Makeover," said Nesta.

"Who's the poor victim this time?"

Nesta looked at me. I looked back at the floor.

Tony got up and started dancing in front of me. "'Don't go changing, tryin' to please me . . .'"

"Go and see Mum, Tony," said Nesta. "It's time for your medication."

"So what was all that about?" I asked Lucy. The four of us were sitting on the bus on our way over to my house later that morning. "You know, Tony?"

Lucy shrugged. "We used to go out. Then we finished. Then we got back together. I don't know where we are now."

"Muswell Hill," teased Nesta as the bus went up the Broadway past Marks & Spencer.

"He adores you," said Izzie.

"That's part of the problem," said Lucy. "See, we're just getting on great, then he starts again"— she caressed the air with her hands—"with wandering hands. I'm not ready for all that yet. I want it to be special when I go further with a boy. I don't want to do it because I feel pressured that if I don't, he'll dump me for someone who puts out more easily. You know?"

I nodded. No, I didn't know. I hadn't even been *snogged* yet.

"And you saw what he's like,' said Lucy. "Flirting with you . . ."

"Oh, I never . . . ," I started. "I would never . . . I mean he *is* gorgeous, there's no denying that, but . . ."

"Oh, don't worry, T. J., he's like that with all girls. That's another reason why I don't give in to the wandering hands. I'd never feel as if I could trust him."

"Well, no reason to worry about me. You saw what I was like back there. Always the same when there are decent boys around. I told you, I go *stupid*. You know there's that book *Men are from Mars, Women are from Venus*. Well, I want to write one, *Men are from Mars, Women are from Venus, Teenagers are from Planet Zog*."

"Good idea," said Lucy.

"It's mad," I continued, "because, I want to be a writer but, well, I told you my problem with finding the right words at the right time. Why do they always come after, like when I'm falling asleep or something?"

"That's good, it means your subconscious mind is working on it," said Izzie. "I find that with my lyrics. You have to consider the words. Play with them until you've got them right. Let them come to you sometimes. It can happen in the middle of the night. I'd say that is the sign that you *will* be a writer."

"And if you're from Planet Zog," said Lucy, "you can always write science fiction."

I laughed and punched her arm. "I wish I could be more like you, Nesta. I wish I could come out with great one-liners or put-downs."

"*We* all wish she'd be more like *you*," said Lucy with a grin. "Think before she speaks, sometimes."

"It does get me in trouble," said Nesta. "Sometimes."

"So, at last," said Lucy as we got to our gate. "We get to meet the man of the moment."

"Who? Scott?" I said, glancing up at his bedroom window to see if he'd seen us. "He usually goes out Saturday mornings."

"No, silly. Not Scott," said Lucy, pointing at the downstairs window next to our front door where a furry face was looking out. "Mojo."

I laughed as I unlocked the door and was almost knocked over as he leaped up to say hello.

"I've only been away a night," I said as he licked my face then ran round the girls, sniffing then rolling on the floor, his tail wagging madly.

After they'd all made a huge fuss over him, we all trooped up to my bedroom.

"Fab garden," said Nesta, looking out of the

window. "It's huge and *wow*, a hammock. How cool. You've got visitors though. On the patio, your gran and grandad are here."

I went over to look out.

"Er, no," I said, pulling back. "That's my mum and dad."

Nesta looked like she wanted to die.

"Mum had me late, when she was in her mid-forties."

"Oh, *très* Cherie Blair," said Izzie, going for a look.

"No," said Nesta. "*Très* Jerry Hall. Much more glam. Now let's look in your wardrobe."

And that was it. No problem. *Très* Jerry Hall and show us your clothes. I needn't have worried at all.

"I hope I didn't offend," said Nesta as she held up baggy tracksuit bottoms and put them on the reject pile. "You know, calling them your grandparents."

"No prob. I know they're ancient. In fact I call them the Wrinklies."

"I nicknamed my step-father The Lodger when he first arrived," said Izzie, flopping on the bed next to Mojo. "I couldn't relate to him any other way, although we get on better now. But the thought of him sharing a bed with Mum, you know, *eew.* . . ."

"Huh," said Lucy. "You think you've got problem parents? Mine get the prize. Why can't they be normal instead of mad hippies? They're so embarrassing sometimes."

"My brother's a hippie. You know, the one who's abroad. I could introduce him to your mum and dad when he's back."

"Yeah," said Lucy. "They could have a soy bean party or something and talk about vegan shoes."

"Vegan shoes?" I asked.

"Plastic. No leather. Dad sells them at the shop."

"I think your mum and dad are great," said Izzie. "I really like them."

"Well that's because you are a *very* strange person," said Lucy.

Izzie retaliated by throwing a cushion at her.

Not wanting to be left out, Nesta grabbed one of my pillows and bashed both of them over the head with it. "Oh, be*have*," she said in her best Mike Myers voice.

Both of them picked up cushions and began pelting her.

If you can't beat them, join them, I thought as I reached for a second pillow.

It was hysterical. Even Mojo joined in, jumping on whomever he could and barking his head off.

Five minutes later Lucy was face down on the floor with Izzie sitting on her back. Izzie was tickling her under her arms. "Repent, repent. Say I am the most fab fabster in the world, no, the *universe*."

"Never," cried Lucy into the carpet.

Whilst they battled it out on the floor, Nesta and I were using my bed as a trampoline.

"I'm Xena, Warrior Princess," cried Nesta as she leaped in the air and whacked me over the head with a pillow.

"And *I'm* Buffy the Vampire Slayer," I yelled as I delivered a nifty whack to her knees. "*Die*, you pathetic imbecile."

Just at that second, my bedroom door opened.

"What in *heaven's* name is that din?" shouted Dad above the racket. "It sounds as if someone's being murdered."

We all froze on the spot as if playing a game of statues.

Dad was definitely in Scary Dad mode and I

prayed he wasn't going to make a scene.

"Aren't you a bit old for this tomfoolery?" he asked.

Nesta and I got off the bed and Lucy and Izzie got up off the floor. We stood in line, looking sheepish and not knowing what to do next. Lucy was staring at the floor, Izzie was grinning at my father like an idiot, and Nesta was looking at her nails, trying to pretend that she wasn't there.

Then I noticed Lucy's shoulders going up and down in silent laughter. This set me off. Then Izzie. Then Nesta, as all of us exploded into a fit of laughing.

Dad looked to the heavens in exasperation. "*Fourteen*, T.J. Isn't it about time you started acting like a young woman?'

I nodded furiously, but tears were falling down my cheeks.

"I'm going to my club for a bit of *peace*," said Dad, going out and slamming the door behind him.

"Oops," I said, then started sniggering. "Iz, Lucy, Nesta meet my dad. Oh dear . . ."

"Sorrysorry," said Nesta. Then she picked up one of my bras from a pile of ironing on the desk and put it on over her T-shirt.

"Guess we're going to have to work on our

refined and well-behaved bit, huh?" she said, sticking her chest out.

I nodded. "Demure and wotsit," I said, picking a pair of knickers from the pile and putting them on my head.

"And vewee vewee mature," said Lucy in a little girlie voice as she sprang up on my bed and jumped up as high as she could.

---

e-mail: Inbox (4)
From: hannahnutter@fastmail.com
To: goody2shoes@psnet.co.uk
Date: 22 June
Subject: Cape Town boy babe

Mambo bandana baby. Bin bisy bee. Fabola barbie last night and I have neeews. I met a boy. I seriously think he may be the One. I may even have to phone you for a yabayaba. He is Drop Dead Divine. A bronzed Adonis. His name is Luke. We had devine tucker and deep talk.

H X

P.S. Luke (swoon swoon) has a book title for you. *Romantic Fantasies* by Everly Night. Heehee. Double arf.

From: hannahnutter@fastmail.com
To: goody2shoes@psnet.co.uk
Date: 22 June
Subject: Scary Dad

Where are you? I phoned and got Scary Dad who said you were at a sleepover. Then he grilled me about whether my mum and dad knew I was phoning. Don't dare phone again. Get thine holy finger out and e-mail me as SOOON as you get in. Loooooooooaaaaaaaaaaads to tell you.

Hx

From: hannahnutter@fastmail.com
To: goody2shoes@psnet.co.uk
Date: 23 June
Subject: Alert alert. Lost T. J. Watts.

Okela. Ista no joke no more. *Ou est* you? *Ou Ou OU?*

Hx

From: paulwatts@worldnet.com
To: goody2shoes@psnet.co.uk
Date: 23 June
Subject: hols

Hey, little sis. Hope it's all going well and Scary Dad not giving you too hard a time. Life here is truly wonderful. Did a day with a holy man, amazing as he is out here in India, but is really from Kilburn. Lots of stuff happening with my third eye. Plus he's re-energized my chakras.

Did two-day meditation session with holy man. Nice group. All gelled well. Fairy-story landscapes and sunsets. Friendly people but Saskia has got amoebic dysentery.

Rock on. Stay true.

Paul

PS Please can you ask Ma to go to the Embassy and get me a new passport. Mine was nicked when I slept on the beach the other night. Ta. Plus some peppermint oil and sulphur and pulsatilla homeopathic stuff for the runs.

e-mail: Outbox (1)
From: goody2shoes@psnet.co.uk
To: hannahnutter@fastmail.com
Date: 23 June
Subject: Friday night

Hey H

Glad you met boy. Luke. I want *details*. Height? Weight? Snogged yet? Level of snogging? Marks out of ten for snogging? etc.

Me had fabola time at sleepover with Nesta, Izzie, and Lucy. Nesta's bro is divine, but taken by Lucy. Sort of. He has wandering hands apparently, which Nesta says is a disease a lot of boys in North London suffer from. She's going to do a makeover on me for the magazine. Before/after kind of thing. They all came over to go through my wardrobe but couldn't find anything. *Quelle* surprise. Oh and Mum bought me the dress from hell. Lucy said I had to be honest with Mum so I was and she's given me the receipt so I can change it. Thank de Lord. After we'd been through my wardrobe, we went into the garden as we are having uno heat wave here. It was nice and relaxed as Dad had gone to his club for A BIT OF PEACE. (He caught us being *un peu* silly and making a lot of noise and well, you know what he can be like.) Nesta had a go on the hammock under the cherry trees. Scott came running over the minute he spotted her from his bedroom window. He leaped over the fence with a flower, trying to impress her, but he gave her the shock of her life and she fell out of the hammock. Then Mojo jumped all over her. It was very funny. Scott was all over her, all dopey with big cow eyes. I felt a bit jealous, although I know that she has a boyfriend and she said after that Scott wasn't her type. Still. I wish a boy would be all over me. I think I may be the only girl in our class who hasn't been snogged. Maybe I'll never get a boy ever. Maybe I'm just not the sort boys like.

T. J.

e-mail: Inbox (1)
From: hannahnutter@fastmail.com
To: goody2shoes@psnet.co.uk
Date: 23 June
Subject: you don't 'alf talk rubbish sometimes

T. J.

You're not the only girl who's never been snogged in Year Nine. I know for a fact that Joanne Richards and Mo Harrison haven't been and unless Mo sorts out her halitosis, she never will be.

Luke. Height 6ft at least. Blonde. Body like a god. Snogged, yes. Level 3. Okay, 4. Well, he is a god. Marks out of ten for snoggability? 9. But practice will make perfect.

I think it's great, those girls doing a makeover. You are gorgeous, but don't make the most of yourself. I've always said this. I like the sound of Nesta, Iz, and Lucy and often thought that if I hadn't been friends with you, I would like to have been friends with them.

Tata for now

Hannah. South African goddess of luurve

Books: Are you still doing this?

Run to the Loo by Willie Makeit

Chapter 10

My
Fair Lady.
Not

"You'll never do it," I said, beginning to feel desperate. "It's hopeless. I am Ugly Git from Uglygitland."

"Roma wasna builta in a day," said Nesta, tugging her way through my hair.

"The darkest hour is just before dawn," said Lucy, who was kneeling on the floor next to me, retouching my nails.

"Suppose," I said, looking gloomily at my reflection in the mirror in Nesta's bedroom. My hair was a frizzy mess. I had an aloe-vera face mask on that made me look like a ghost and a big spot threatening to erupt on my chin.

"Lack of self-esteem," said Izzie. "That's your problem, T. J. You are a babe, but you don't know it. Look, you have fabulous hair that you always scrape back in a plait, long *long* legs that you never show, a fab figure that you hide in baggy tracksuits, and a great mouth that all those thin-lipped models who have collagen injections would die for."

Always one to accept compliments graciously, I said, "Humphh. And you clearly have the observational skills of a brain-dead gnat."

We'd already done the "before" shot in the morning at Lucy's house. Steve had offered to be photographer with his new camera and it was hysterical. I'd worn the "dress from hell" that Mum had bought me, and Izzie had done my hair in two bunches high on either side of my head. Lucy had stuck dog hair from Ben and Jerry's brush onto my legs with Evostick so that I'd look like I had hairy legs. (I put my foot down when she got carried away and tried to stick some on my upper lip to give me a moustache though.) And Nesta had given me some lessons in bad posture so I looked even more frumpy.

"All beautiful women have great posture," she'd said. "It's one of the first things they teach at modeling school. To stand up straight. So for these shots, stoop, like you have round shoulders."

Lucy raided her mum's jumble sale bargain bags and produced some seriously tasteless jewelry. Big dangly earrings and an Indian necklace.

"But they don't go with the dress," I'd said.

The girls had looked at me as if I was stupid.

"And the object of this exercise *is*?" said Nesta.

By the time they'd finished, I looked like a sack of old potatoes. With hairy legs.

"You look awful," Steve'd said approvingly when I came down the stairs, then walked across the hallway like a duck. A round-shouldered duck.

"Yeah, like Waynetta Slob from Harry Enfield's show," laughed Lal.

"I want to do the shots round the back garden near the trash cans," said Steve.

"What, like I'm on the scrap heap?" I asked.

Steve gave me a look as if to say "yeah", then he grinned. "You don't look that bad," he said. "It's only that dress that makes you look like a frump."

"But the trash cans in the background give a sort of subliminal message, like I'm a load of rubbish," I said.

"Yeah," said Steve. "Exactly. We've been doing it in film class, all about how surrounding images register with the subconscious and can reinforce what you're trying to say without people realizing."

"What are you on about?" said Lucy. She did an enormous yawn as though bored out of her mind, but I found what he was saying interesting.

We had a great laugh as Steve clicked away and I assumed the most unattractive positions and facial expressions I could.

At one point, Mr. and Mrs. Lovering came out to see what we were up to. They watched for a moment as I cavorted for the camera doing my sumo-wrestler position, then a bit of karate chopping. They looked very puzzled to hear Steve say in a French accent, "And look as miserable as you can. Like your durg 'as just died and gone to durgee 'eaven *avec les autres chiens*. That's it. *Eh bien. Marvelleuse, mon ooglee légume. . . . Diable* mon sooth, chins up, chins down. *Mais oui, bien sûr. Degoûtantamont*."

Clearly languages were not his thing, I thought, as his parents both shrugged and went back into the house.

The second part of the makeover wasn't a laugh. Oh no-ho, not at all. The girls were taking it seriously. As in *mega*-seriously. They were on a blooming makeover mission.

I was plucked, waxed, massaged, moisturized, conditioned, manicured, pedicured, blow-dried, made up, made over, and dressed.

"Okay, you can look now," said Nesta, removing her dressing gown from the mirror where she'd draped it so I couldn't see.

The reflection of a brunette Barbie doll gazed back at me. I was wearing one of Nesta's dresses, a short pale blue number and her mum's Jimmy Choo gray strappy heels. Nesta had given me "big" hair, loose and flowing over my shoulders, and Lucy had made up my face with a little shadow, blusher, and rusty lipstick.

"You shall go to the ball, Cinders," said Nesta. "You look fab."

"Yeah, a top babe," said Lucy. "Do you like it?"

I wasn't sure. I did look good. And I had to admit that my legs looked really long. But I wasn't sure that looking like such a girlie girl was me. Mind you, I didn't know what *was* me.

"What do you think, Izzie?"

"Watch out boys," she sang. "There's a new kid in town."

Nesta's mum gave us a lift to Hampstead High Street where we were meeting Steve to do the "after" shots.

She dropped us halfway down Heath Street and as we got out of the car, someone did a long wolf whistle. I looked over to where it was coming from and there was Scott. He was with a bunch of his mates sitting at a table outside Café Nero.

"T. J. Watts. *Cor* bloody cor," he said as he looked me up and down and then up and down again, his eyes finally resting on my legs. "You're a *girl.*"

"*Uhyuh,*" I said as I noticed all the other boys round the table also ogling me. I felt exposed standing there in my shorter-than-short dress and I wasn't sure I liked the attention I was getting. Everyone was staring and there was nowhere to hide. Even an old bloke in his forties was gawping as he went by. Served him right, I thought, when he walked smack into a woman with her dog and got all tangled up in the lead.

Scott took my hand and introduced us to his friends. He seemed to be enjoying himself immensely. Then he was all over Nesta and acting like he'd known her for ever. All his mates sniggered when she dismissed him saying, "In your dreams."

He didn't seem to mind though. In fact, I think he took it as a come-on.

Lucy spotted Steve coming down the street and waved. He waved back and, when he saw me, he did a slow whistle under his breath.

"See they've done a number," he said.

"Wow," I said to Izzie as we walked or rather they walked and I tottered. "Is it really this simple? A bit of lipstick, high heels, show your legs and boys turn to jelloid?"

Izzie nodded. "And even more so if you show a bit of cleavage. It's amazing to watch. Hysterical. You see boys' cheekbones twitching with the effort not to look at your chestie bits, but their eyes keep zinging back there as if pulled by an invisible magnet."

"Not a problem I have," said Lucy, "being a thirty-two triple A myself."

"Lucy's bros call her Nancy-No-Tits," confided Nesta.

"We can't all be Dolly Parton like you," laughed Lucy, punching her arm.

We went down to the bottom of Heath Street with Scott and his mates trailing after us and sat at a table outside House on the Hill. Nesta ordered drinks and Steve took some shots as he said he wanted them to look natural rather than posed. This time I didn't have to do much, he did all work. He was much quieter this time, not acting as loony mad as he had been in the morning. He wasn't as much fun. In fact he seemed to want to get it over with, as though he'd lost interest.

"Why did you choose Hampstead for the 'after' shots?" I asked, in an attempt to get him talking.

"Trendy place. It's glam. Rich," he said, then he clamped up again.

He didn't hang around after he'd got his photos

and muttered something about having to get back to finish homework.

Something had clearly upset him since this morning. He was really subdued. I must ask Lucy if she knows.

---

e-mail: Outbox (1)
From: goody2shoes@psnet.co.uk
To: hannahnutter@fastmail.com
Date: 24 June
Subject: The new *moi*

Hey Hannahlooloo

Had brill time today with makeover. Steve took photos on his new camera. Will send copies. Nesta made me look very girlie girl but not sure it's me. Felt uncomfortable for a few reasons. I never realized before that you can be invisible in big baggy clothes and no one takes too much notice. It's kind of safe. But going out in Hampstead today, everyone was staring. I felt exposed. Nesta said to "strut my stuff, girlfriend," but people act differently to you if you do. Girls can be bitchy. Boys disturbed. Scott went all googly-eyed at me. But mainly people stared. I wasn't sure if I liked it. Talking of

---

which, we bumped into Wendy Roberts coming out of Accessorize. She did a double take when she saw me and almost spat out her Magnum. Then she said that dressed like I was, I should go far, the further the better. I wasn't sure what to make of her reaction.

Spika soon

Love, T. J.

P.S. Yes, yes. More book titles, as I'm definitely going to put some in the mag. *Body Parts* by Anne Atomy

---

e-mail: Inbox (2)

From: hannahnutter@fastmail.com

To: goody2shoes@psnet.co.uk

Date: 24 June

Subject: The noo *vous*

Ole *le* noodley noodles baby

I think the word to describe Wendy's reaction is *envy*. God, I wish I'd been there to see her. And you. I do miss Hampstead and Highgate and hanging out. I bet you looked the business. Don't worry about looking girlie. You'll find your style. Today was just the beginning of T. J. as Sex Queen of North London. Remember Confucius he say, "Every journey start with first step. That is, unless step going sideways or backward."

Have been to Luke's posh pad *avec* pool this weekend. Some consolation for missing Ingerlandie.

May your flobbalots be mighty

HannahXXXXXXXXXXXXXXXXXXXXXXXXXXXXXXX

From: hannahnutter@fastmail.com
To: goody2shoes@psnet.co.uk
Date: 24 June
Subject: d'oh. Steve?????

Er *exscooth* me?? But I just re-read your e-mail. Have you been holding out on me? More about Steve? Details? Height? Weight? Fanciability? Etc etc.
Immediatetment.

e-mail: Outbox (1)
From: goody2shoes@psnet.co.uk
To: hannahnutter@fastmail.com
Date: 24 June
Subject: d'oh. Steve?????

Gordy flobbalots. I told you already. *Lucy's* older
brother. Fanciability. I guess he's nice-looking, but
not in a drop-dead way like Scott, who I think I
may be in love with. And at last he's noticed I am a
girl. It's different with Steve. He's easy to talk to. I
don't go peculiar when he's around. He's a mate.
     T. J.

   Book: *Strange Breasts* by Won Hung Low

---

e-mail: Inbox (1)
From: hannahnutter@fastmail.com
To: goody2shoes@psnet.co.uk
Date: 24 June
Subject: d'oh. Steve?????

Zoot allors. Snog him anyway and get in some practice!

   HXXXX

   Book: *Drink Problems* by Imorf Mihead

Chapter 11

Walking the Durg

"Don't go into the woods," said Mum as I got ready to take Mojo for a walk on Wednesday after school. "Stay on the roads where people can see you."

"I'm going to ask if Scott will come," I said. "Then it will be okay, won't it?"

"Yes, fine," said Mum. "But don't be too late back. You've still got homework to do."

I couldn't wait to call on Scott. I'm sure it wasn't my imagination that he'd been so flirty in Hampstead on Saturday. He'd seemed genuinely bowled over by my new look and at one point he'd held my hand and squeezed it. I'd got that lovely fluttery feeling again, like when he'd nuzzled my neck. I couldn't stop thinking about it and what it might be like to hold his hand again and even kiss him. My insides went all liquidy and peculiar just imagining it.

I combed my hair loose, put on a bit of lipstick, then put Mojo on his lead and went next door.

Mrs. Harris answered.

"Is Scott home?" I asked, trying my best not to give away the fact I was quaking. Mad really, as I'd been over to his house a million times and thought nothing of it.

She called up to him in his room and he emerged at the top of the stairs a few minutes later.

"Oh, hi, T. J."

"Er. Hi. Um. I'm taking Mojo for a walk. Do you want to come?"

He shook his head. "Watching *The Simpsons*," he said.

"Oh. Okay, cool. Another time," I said, hoping that I hadn't shown how disappointed I was. He didn't even come down to say good-bye.

As Mojo and I went up to Muswell Hill Broadway, I wondered if I'd misread the signals.

Had he ever held my hand before? Or squeezed it? I couldn't remember. Maybe I was reading too much into it. Maybe he hadn't liked my new look after all. But he seemed to at the time. He kept staring at me. I felt so confused.

I decided I'd look in a few shop windows in the hope of finding an alternative style to Barbie babe. Fat chance, I thought, as I looked at the various tops and skirts on display. I wasn't sure what I wanted to look like, though one thing I was certain about was that I didn't want to wear those high heel things again. Agony. They may have looked good, but there was only so far I was prepared to go in the have-to-suffer-to-be-beautiful game.

Mojo trotted alongside me happily as I pondered the great philosophical question of who was the real T. J. Watts.

Is she Noola the Alien girl?

Or Miss Strop-Bossy Prefect who likes to put boys straight?

Or Arm Wrestling Champion of North London?

Or Miss Goody 2 Shoes who always does her homework?

Or Norma Know-It-All?

Or Barbie's brunette sister?

Or on the other hand, is she a total nutter with loads of different characters living in her head?

"What do you think, Mojo?" I asked as we made our way past the cinema and down Muswell Hill High Road.

"Aha," said a voice behind me. "Talking to yourself, first sign of insanity."

I turned and there was Steve with Ben and Jerry.

"I was talking to Mojo," I said. "But you might be right about the insanity bit. In fact I was just thinking I might well be going bonkers."

He laughed. "You going to Highgate Woods?" he asked as Mojo, Ben, and Jerry got down to the dignified business of sniffing each other's bottoms.

"No," I said. "Mojo would love to, but Mum said I mustn't go on my own."

Steve checked his watch. "Well, we have just been, but I've no doubt these guys wouldn't object to a bit longer. Come on, I'll keep you company."

I gave Mum a quick ring on my mobile and, after giving me the third degree, she finally agreed.

We set off for the woods and once inside, let the dogs off their leads. They raced off excitedly, best of friends already. As they charged about, Steve and I chatted like old mates. It's so weird, I thought. Here's me, all great pals with Steve and nervous with Scott, whereas only a week ago, Scott was my pal and Steve was a complete stranger.

"So, what's with you and that guy?" asked Steve after a while.

"What guy?"

"One outside Café Nero. You seemed to like him."

"God, am I *that* obvious?" I was taken aback that he'd read my thoughts. "I hope he didn't notice."

"I don't think he did. Too busy ogling Nesta."

My heart sank. Maybe that was it. It was really Nesta he was interested in. And he'd been doing the flirty bit to get to her through me.

"I know," I said. "He lives next door to me. Has done for years and we've always been mates. Until lately. It's all changed. I found myself . . . you know, er, well, thinking about him a lot. I don't know what I feel, it's all so weird. And I certainly don't know what he thinks, but I don't think he rates me other than someone to talk to. Oh, I don't know. . . ."

"Any boy who doesn't fancy you must be mad," said Steve. "And I'll tell you one of the biggest secrets about boys. . . ."

I held my breath for the great revelation.

"They're exactly the same as girls in that they also feel shy and awkward that they don't always say the right thing or act the right way."

"Really?"

Steve looked at me closely. "Boys may act confident but can be just as nervous as you underneath. Everyone fears being turned down and looking a fool."

"I just don't think he's interested. . . ."

"How do you know who's interested or not?" said Steve. "Sometimes when a boy is acting disinterested, it's actually more frozen than cool. Frozen with fear as mostly girls call the shots. Boys fear rejection like anyone else."

Me calling the shots? That was a laugh. But boys being nervous too, that was obvious really. I'd never thought about it before. I'd been so caught up in my own ill-ease, I hadn't thought about theirs. Of course boys must feel that way too sometimes.

"For instance," said Steve, "you may think a boy doesn't want to know, but he may be too scared to say anything. I know I am sometimes, you know, if I like someone."

Maybe that's what Scott had been doing just now, I thought. Acting cool. Afraid I'd reject him. No. Not possible. Or was it? I felt more confused than ever.

"In fact . . . ," said Steve.

"How does anyone ever get together then?" I interrupted. "I think I'd need someone to make it *very* clear to me."

"How?"

"Dunno. Cards. Presents. Billboard in Piccadilly? Shout from the top of the rooftops I FANCY T. J. WATTS."

Steve laughed. "I'm sure there are loads of boys after you," he said. "You just don't know it."

"Really?"

"Well you saw the reaction you were getting yesterday."

"Yeah. But I wasn't sure if that girlie-girl look was really my style."

Steve nodded. "Yeah. Don't get me wrong, but

I thought Nesta had made you into a Nesta clone. That look suits her, but I see you more as Buffy than Barbie."

"Really?" Cool, I thought. I liked the sound of that. More Buffy than Barbie. I must make a note of what kind of clothes she wears.

"So how's the mag going?"

"Okay. But it's brought out the competitive side of everyone at school. And some of them can be pretty bitchy. Like there's this one girl, the one we saw in Hampstead. She's giving me a really hard time." I continued filling him in on the Dog of the Week stunt that Wendy had pulled. "Wendy Roberts."

Steve slapped his forehead. "The one outside Accessorize? I *knew* I knew her. Now you say the name . . . A mate of mine went out with her." Then he chuckled. "I could tell you some good goss about her."

"What?"

"No front teeth."

"How do you know?"

"My mate found out when he snogged her. One of them came loose. That's how I remember her name. She's waiting for implants, but the dentist won't do them until she's older. So she's got dentures. Real false teeth. Apparently she knocked both of them out in a riding accident. You could print a piece about dentists. And put in a picture of her as an example."

I laughed at the thought of it. "With a caption: All I want for Christmas is my two front teeth."

"Or instead of 'wide-eyed and legless,' you could write, 'wide-eyed and toothless.'"

"Don't tempt me," I said.

The time whizzed by as we chatted on about ideas for the school newspaper and Steve offered to do a piece on photography.

When I looked at my watch, it said eight o'clock.

"God, I'd better go," I said. "Mum'll kill me."

We rounded up the dogs, put them back on their leads, and Steve walked me to the top of our road.

"So, bye," he said as we reached our gate.

"Bye."

He went to go, then turned back.

"Er. Um. Do you . . . would you like to play tennis one day?"

"Sure," I said. I'd enjoyed the time we spent together and was beginning to think we could be good mates. "If you're prepared to be beaten."

---

e-mail: Outbox (2)
From: goody2shoes@psnet.co.uk
To: paulwatts@worldnet.com
Date: 25 June
Subject: runs

Dear Bro

Sorry to hear about the amoebic dysentery. Have asked Mum to get you another passport and get it sent to you. Haven't told Dad. Be careful.

Love,

T. J.
XXXXXXXXXXXXXXXXXXXXXXXXXXXXXXXXXXXXXXX

From: goody2shoes@psnet.co.uk
To: nestahotbabe@retro.co.uk
Date: 27 June
Subject: movie

Do you fancy the new Julia Roberts movie on
Friday? It's on at the Hollywood Bowl. Lucy and Izzie
are up for it. Hope you can come.

   T. J.
XXXXXXXXXXXXXXXXXXXXXXXXXXXXXXXXXXXXXXXXXX

---

e-mail: Inbox (1)
From: goody2shoes@psnet.co.uk
To: nestahotbabe@retro.co.uk
Date: 27 June
Subject: movie

Cool. I'll be dere.

Chapter 12

More Buffy than Barbie

To do:

1) Watch Buffy videos to note clothes.
2) Return Dress From Hell and swap for something the Buffster would wear.
3) Go to movie wearing new outfit.

It worked.

"T. J., you look wicked," said Izzie as we walked from the bus stop toward the Hollywood Bowl the following Friday. "Your hair looks so much better now you leave it loose, and I love the combats."

Lucy looked me up and down and nodded her approval. "Yeah. And I'm glad to see you haven't ruined the effect by hiding in a big baggy fleece. The tank top is great."

"Yeah. Bootylicious," said Nesta.

I *think* that means she approves.

We made our way through the car park to the cinema and it felt great. I could see groups of lads ogling us. And not just Nesta this time. Even I was getting a few looks.

When we got to the foyer, Izzie and Lucy went off to get the tickets while Nesta and I went upstairs and queued up for popcorn. As we were standing in line, I noticed Scott standing at the top of the escalator on his own. He kept checking his watch and looking down toward the entrance as if he was waiting for someone.

After we'd gotten our popcorn, Scott was still standing on his own, so we found Lucy and Izzie, then made our way over to him.

"Been stood up?" asked Nesta.

Lucy punched her arm. *"Nesta!"*

"What?" said Nesta. *"What?"*

"Actually," said Scott, his face brightening

immediately. "I was waiting for you."

"As *if*," said Nesta, tossing her hair.

Scott checked downstairs then, seeing no one was coming up, he linked his arm through hers. "Looks like my mate has been held up, so the honor of keeping me company is yours."

"Mate or *date* been held up?" asked Nesta. "Admit it. You've been stood up."

Lucy punched her arm again. "Excuse my *rude* friend," she said to Scott. "We don't often let her out at night."

Scott grinned. "So, you coming then?" he said to Nesta before turning to the rest of us. "Sorry, girls. Only got dosh for two tickets."

Nesta took his arm out of hers and came to stand behind us.

"Actually," she said. "I already have plans. With people who actually bother to turn up. Come on, girls. I'm going to the ladies'."

Scott looked taken aback as we walked off leaving him standing there. As I looked over my shoulder, I couldn't help but feel sorry for him. I know him well enough to recognize that what we'd just witnessed was a huge act of bravado.

Everything Steve said to me yesterday came flooding back. How hard it is for boys to take rejection even if they don't show it. It still hurts. His date hadn't shown and Nesta had made a fool of him on top of everything else.

As we stood in front of the mirrors doing our hair and lippie and stuff, I made up my mind.

"I'm going to ask if Scott would like me to go with him to a movie."

"No," chorused Izzie, Lucy and Nesta.

"Why not? He's been let down. He probably feels lousy."

"Who? Scott? Nah, he's well sure of himself," said Nesta. "He thinks he's God's gift and could probably do with being brought down a peg or two."

"No, he's really sweet underneath. It's all an act," I said.

"Ah," sighed Lucy. "Love is blind."

"Well, you don't want to be too easy if you really like him," said Iz. "You need to play hard to get. Boys like the chase."

"But I feel sorry for him," I said. "I'm going to go and ask him."

"How can someone with so many brains be so stupid?" asked Nesta as Lucy sighed in exasperation.

"You can think what you like," I said as I did a last check of my appearance. "But I've known him longer than you and this is something I have to do."

With that, I turned on my heel. As the loo door closed behind me, I could hear Lucy telling Nesta off for being insensitive.

"Yeah. Okay, then," said Scott when I told him that I'd keep him company. "But I'm not going to see the same movie as your mates."

"But Izzie already got me a ticket."

"I'm not sitting anywhere near that lesbian."

"Lesbian?"

"Nesta."

I laughed. Sour grapes, I thought, but I didn't say anything. He was just lashing out because she'd humiliated him in front of the rest of us.

There were five other films on at the complex so I let him pick what we were going to see. He chose a sci-fi film.

"I'm not mad on sci-fi," I said. "Are you sure you don't want to see the new comedy with Julia Roberts? I've heard it's a real laugh. And we can sit on the other side from the girls."

"No way," said Scott. "The sci-fi or I'm going home."

In the end, I gave in. I didn't mind. What I really wanted was a chance to spend some time with Scott alone and see what happened.

Scott loved the film, but I couldn't concentrate. As the screen filled with manic scenes from intergalactic wars, I was only aware of the proximity of Scott. Our knees and elbows touched a couple of times and I was hoping that he would hold my hand, but he just stuffed his face with popcorn.

Maybe real life isn't like the movies, I thought, as another alien got his three heads ripped off, squirting green blood all over the hero. Maybe in real life romance isn't beautiful sunsets and gentle kisses. Maybe in real life romance is sitting in the dark wondering if the boy you're with is *ever* going to make a move that isn't him merely shifting position in his seat. Maybe romance is all fantasy. For the last few days, that's all I'd done. Every night before I went to sleep, I imagined my first kiss with Scott. First he'd push a lock of hair behind my ear, then look deeply into my eyes, then softly press his lips on mine and . . .

A *phwt* noise beside me disturbed my thoughts.

Scott had farted.

"Oops," he said with a grin. "Popcorn-flavored."

After the movie, we made our way out back into the foyer and Scott was a few steps in front of me. Suddenly he spotted a few of his mates who had been with him in Hampstead on the day of the photo shoot.

One of them came over.

"You're the girl who was having her photo taken the other day, aren't you?" he asked.

I nodded.

"You looked really good," he said.

"Thanks."

Suddenly Scott took my hand.

"Yeah, this is T. J.," he said as he introduced the group of boys.

Then he put his arm round me. "Just been to see *Alien Mutants in Cyberspace*," he said, then winked at them. "Didn't get to see much of the film, though, if ya know what I mean. . . ."

The boys sniggered knowingly.

"Anyway, got to go," said Scott and looked at me fondly. "The night is young."

"Yeah, right," said one of the boys as Scott pulled me away.

What was going on? I wondered. Did he fancy me after all and, as Steve said, had been acting cool? Or was this all a big act to make his mates think we were on a date? He still had hold of my hand as we went down the escalator and out the foyer but, unlike the day in Hampstead, I wasn't feeling all fluttery inside. I felt muddled. I didn't want to take my hand away though, as I remembered what he'd said about the night being young. Things could only get better.

When we got outside, I suggested we go and have a cappuccino.

"Got no money left," he said.

"No prob. My treat."

Scott shrugged. "Okay, then. And a hot dog?"

"Fine," I said.

"With onions."

"Fine."

For the next half hour, he talked. I listened.

He talked.

He talked.

I listened.

I was bursting to tell him all about my last few weeks. E-mails from Hannah and Paul. The magazine. My new mates. So much had happened, but I couldn't get a word in edgeways. He talked, I listened. That was the deal and always has been since I'd known him. I'd just never been bothered about it before. As I tried to appear interested, I thought that even Mojo was more interested in what I had to say. And he's a dog.

"So, enough about me. What about you?" he said, finally pausing for breath. "What do you think of me?"

Then he laughed like he'd said the funniest thing ever.

I couldn't help but think how easy Steve had been to talk to. We'd never shut up the other day in the park. But with him, it had been equal. I talked, he listened. He talked, I listened. He'd seemed interested in what I had to say and what my opinions were.

I took a long look at Scott. No doubt he was mucho cute to look at. A lovely curly mouth and deep-brown eyes. But as I stared into them, I thought, Scott Harris, I've never realized this before but you are boring. As in B. O. R. *iiing*.

I had a sudden urge to go home, talk to Mojo, e-mail Hannah, and even maybe catch up with Steve. He had promised to start work on his article for the magazine and I could call to see how it was coming along.

We got the bus home together and when we got to our houses, Scott did a quick check up and down the street, then up at the windows. I was about to go in when he suddenly pushed me against the wall and the next thing I knew I was being snogged.

My first snog.

Ugh. Agh, I thought as his mouth crashed into mine. And erlack, onions. His mouth tasted ukky. It was a really wet, slimy kiss, not how I'd imagined it at all.

When he'd finished cleaning my teeth with his

tongue, he stood back, looking really pleased with himself.

"Catcha later," he said, pointing his index finger at me. Then he turned and went inside.

Not if I see you first, I thought as I wiped my mouth on my arm.

A couple of hours later, I was up in my room working on some ideas for the magazine when the phone went.

"T. J., it's Nesta."

"Oh, hi . . . Nes . . ."

"Listen," interrupted Nesta. "I've got something to say to you and I hope you won't take it the wrong way, but, well, that boy Scott . . . he's not the one for you. Don't ask me how I know, I just do. He thinks too much of himself and I know boys like that look pretty, but all they are interested in is themselves. You deserve better. You mustn't be a doormat. You can do better, believe me. It's just you're suffering from low self-esteem, but someone will come along who you'll have a better time with. Who really wants to be with you. Because you are a babe. With brains. Lethal combination as I've said before. And I know you like Scott, and now you're probably going to hate me and not speak to me, but as a friend I felt I had to tell you. T. J., are you there? Do you hate me now? Please say something? Oh, hell bells and poo. Lucy said I shouldn't phone but Izzie said I should. T. J., T. J. . . ?"

I couldn't say anything because I was too busy laughing and I'd put my hand over the phone so she couldn't hear.

"Nesta. I agree."

"You . . . you *what*?"

"Yeah, you're right. Scott Harris. Cute but dull. Dull as dishwater. And . . . he's a bad snogger."

"He *snogged* you!" exclaimed Nesta. "*Ohmigod.* Details."

We spent the next half-hour yabbering about snogs and Nesta told me all about some of her early disasters.

"It's not always like that," she said in the end.

"Phewww," I said. "So there's hope."

"Mucho mucho," said Nesta. "It can be just how you imagined it and better."

When I put down the phone, I felt really happy.

That night, as I fell asleep, a different boy seemed
to have taken Scott's place in my snogging fantasy.

---

e-mail: Outbox (1)
From: babewithbrains@psnet.co.uk
To: nestahotbabe@retro.co.uk
Date: 29 June
Subject: new e-mail

Note new e-mail address. Whatdoyathink?

T. J.

---

e-mail: Inbox (2)
From: nestahotbabe@retro.co.uk
To: babewithbrains@psnet.co.uk
Date: 29 June
Subject: new e-mail

Bootylicious. See you tomorrow P.M. at Lucy's for
the magazine finale.

   Nesta

From: paulwatts@worldnet.com
To: babewithbrains@psnet.co.uk
Date: 29 June
Subject: hol

Hi T. J.

Holiday really not going as planned. Monsoons have hit the resort. Torrential rain so impossible to sleep on beach. Am crashing in a hut with four other travelers, but caught head lice after I borrowed a sleeping bag (mine was nicked). Oh, and to top it all, Saskia has run away with the holy man from Kilburn. I have the runs and mosquito bites as big as golf balls.

Hope all well your end.
Love,

Paul

P.S. Please ask Dad to send very strong medical supplies. Anything and everything.

Chapter 13

The Mad House

The next afternoon, I had half of North London employed as my editorial staff.

At home, I'd asked Mum and Dad each to write something.

"We're theming the magazine toward summer," I said to Dad, "so I'd like you to do some handy hints for traveling abroad from a doctor's point of view. Make it relevant. A mini medical cabinet that you could pack in a suitcase. Stuff for sunburn, mosquitoes, the runs, and so on."

"Will do," he said with a grin.

I think he was really chuffed to have been asked.

And Mum was doing an article on how to deal with exam stress.

"Ten handy hints," I said. "It has to be accessible."

I left them listening to Radio 4 and sipping Earl Grey tea as they worked.

Over at Nesta's, Tony was working on a cartoon for a competition. We were going to invite readers to send in captions and print the best in the next edition. If there *was* a next edition.

At Lucy's, Steve and I worked on the computer in his and Lal's bedroom.

Lucy and Nesta were finishing their articles in the living room.

Izzie was on the computer in Lucy's bedroom, working out horoscopes for the coming month.

Mrs. Lovering kept bringing us herbie drinks with ginseng and some icky-tasting stuff called Guryana.

"Keeps you alert," she said.

And Mr. Lovering sat in the kitchen playing his guitar.

"Music to inspire the workers," he said when I went down to ask for a new ink cartridge for the printer. How a rendition of "You Ain't Nothing but a Hound Dog" was supposed to motivate us, I have no idea, but Ben and Jerry seemed to like it as they joined in, howling away with great gusto.

"This place is a *mad* house," said Lal, looking at his dad with disapproval. "I'm off somewhere normal. Where I can *think* in peace!"

"Go to my house, then," I said. "It's like a morgue."

No one's ever happy with their lot, I thought, as I watched him storm off in a huff. I'm sure Mum and Dad would agree with Lal if they came over, but I loved it. Mr. L. (as Izzie calls him) is a real laugh and as opposite to my dad as anyone you could meet. He's an old hippie who's losing his hair, yet has a ponytail. And he wears very bright Hawaiian shirts and Indian sandals. Mrs. L. is hippie-dippie too, today wearing a Peruvian skirt with mirrors round the hem and a rather strange crocheted top.

"You okay, T. J.?" asked Steve when I went back upstairs. "You're kind of quiet today."

"Yuh, yunewee," I muttered.

A *lot* had happened in the last twenty-four hours. Mainly in my head. I'd had my eyes opened to what a user Scott was, and I was experiencing an almighty twinge of conscience that I'd treated Steve the same way. Someone to earbash with my problems. Only last week I'd been on about how much I fancied Scott and how he never noticed me and treated me like a mate and nothing more. That was *exactly* how I'd treated Steve. And he'd been so sweet, reassuring me that I was fanciable and telling me how boys really felt about girls.

As I sat next to him at the desk, I felt the warmth of his arm against mine and caught the scent of soap on his skin. Back came the old fluttery feeling, only this time, I was with Steve, not Scott. How had I not noticed what nice eyes he had? Kind. Hazel-brown with honey flecks around the iris. And good hands, I thought, as he pressed keys on the computer keyboard—long fingers, elegant.

And it was too late. If I said anything, he'd think I was a complete airhead. Fickle and a half. In love with Scott one week, fancying him the next.

"So have you decided what to do about Wendy Roberts and her dentures?" asked Steve, leaning over me to see what I'd written.

"Er, *yu . . . nu . . . wee . . .* Wendy, yes. I've decided I'm not going to stoop to her level. I'll save stuff like that for my secret notebook and use it later when I write novels."

"Good for you," said Steve. "So do you reckon we'll be ready to hand the mag in on Monday?"

"Nih . . . ing . . . yah . . . ," I said, cursing Alien Girl who had taken over my vocal chords. "Umost. I mean, almost."

Steve was looking at me as though I had two heads.

"Gottask Luceand Nestasomething. Backin aminute," I said, jumping up.

I stumbled downstairs to find Lucy and Nesta. I needed help.

I sat on the floor and put my head in my hands. "Ag. Agh. Agherama."

"Hey, it'll be all right. We're almost there," said Nesta. "We'll do it on time."

"Do what?" I said, looking up.

"The mag."

"Oh it's not that. It's . . ." I looked at Lucy. Steve was her brother. What would *she* think if she knew I'd been fantasizing about him? She knew how I felt about Scott. She'd think I was a complete tart for changing my mind so fast.

"So what is it?" asked Lucy.

"Nothing," I said.

"Yeah, looks like it," said Nesta. "Come on, spill."

I sighed. Then looked at the two of them waiting expectantly. Then I sighed again.

Nesta and Lucy started doing big sighs as well. Then really exaggerating them, heaving huge extended breaths until I had to laugh.

"Okay. Lie out on the sofa," said Lucy.

I did as I was told and Lucy sat at the other end.

"So Miss Vatts. Vat seems to be ze problem?"

I couldn't say. Silence. Big silence. It grew and filled the room.

"Ah. Boy trouble," said Lucy.

"But which boy?" said Nesta. "You're over Scott, *n'est-ce pas?*"

I nodded. "It's another boy who I've only just realized I like. Much nicer than Scott. And now I'm all tongue-tied and stupid around him. And I think I've blown it. And it's probably too late."

"Oh, you mean *Steve?*" asked Lucy.

164

"*How* did you know?"

"Kind of obvious from the start," said Lucy.

"*Obvious? To whom? I've* only just realized. And who knows what's going on in his head. If he likes *me.*"

"Er, *hello*?" said Lucy. "What planet are you on exactly?"

"Planet Zog, actually," I said, and explained all about Noola and her ability to take over my head.

"Well, for your information, Steve hasn't stopped talking about you and asking about you ever since he met you," said Lucy. "And he was well miffed with the fact you fancied Scott. Didn't you notice how weirded out he was when we bumped into Scott in Hampstead?"

"Suppose he was kind of quiet that day. I thought I'd done something to upset him."

"D'oh. *Yeah.* You had," said Lucy. "Fancied someone else."

Izzie came down the stairs and flopped on the sofa.

"Whassup?" she asked.

"T. J.," said Nesta. "She turns into Noola the Alien Girl whenever she fancies a boy. Noola only knows three words. Tell her, T.J."

"*Uhyuh. Yunewee.* And *nihingyah.*"

Lucy started giggling and doing an alien robot impersonation like C-3PO in *Star Wars* up and down the room.

"*Uhyuh,*" she squeaked in a high voice. "*Yunewee. Nihingyaaaah.*"

We were laughing so hard that Steve came down to see what was going on. Of course, I went purple.

"So?" said Steve.

"So noth . . . nothing," chuckled Nesta.

"Just something Lucy said," said Izzie.

Steve looked up to the heavens, then turned to me. "You coming back to finish your editorial?"

"Uh . . . *uhyuh,*" I said, and Lucy exploded with laughter.

Steve heaved a sigh, which Lucy and Nesta copied.

Steve looked at us all as though we were stupid. "*When* you're ready, T. J.," he said, and went back to his room.

"See, do you *see* now?" I said. "I'm going to blow it. And we were getting on so well and now I'm going to act like an idiot around him and he'll think I'm Dork from Dorkland, Nerd from Nerdville, Airhead from . . ."

"Shut the door, Lucy," said Izzie. "We clearly have work to do."

We spent the next twenty minutes doing a visualization with Izzie. She's well into self-help stuff and had been reading in one of her books about positive thinking.

"It's all in the mind," she said. "You can get over this and put Noola the Alien Girl to rest. But you have to see yourself acting confidently. I've been reading all about it for when I do gigs."

"But I think you're either confident or not," I said. "Like Nesta. It's not something you can learn."

"Oh, yes it is," said Nesta. "We all have our own tricks. Sometimes I pretend I'm a character out of a film if I feel nervous. Then I act as I think they would. It really works."

"And I used to be hopeless about singing in public," said Izzie. "So bad I couldn't sleep at night. I used to be well terrified of looking a fool and this has really helped."

"So, you think I could learn to talk sense when I meet a boy I like?"

"Definitely," said Izzie. "In fact, my book says,

"'We are what we repeatedly do. Confidence is not an act but a habit.'" You have to practice."

"Cool," said Lucy. "Sounds good to me. What do we do?"

Izzie made us all sit down and close our eyes. First we had to imagine the situation we felt nervous in, so I thought about being close to Steve upstairs. We had to imagine the room, the surroundings, what we were wearing, all the details.

Then Izzie said, "Imagine yourself being relaxed, calm, and completely in control. Imagine the other person's response to you. In your mind, see them laughing at your jokes, listening with interest to what you say, *liking* you."

She made us imagine the situation over and over again until in my imagination, Steve was gawping at me in open admiration, amazed at my witticisms. In *awe* at my brilliant conversation.

"Okay, open your eyes, everyone."

We did as we were told and looked around at each other.

"How do you feel now, T. J.?"

I stood up and went to the door. "Awesome. Noola. She dead." I put my hands on my hips

Arnold Schwarzeneggar style and said, "I'll be back. *Hasta la vista*, baby."

Nesta laughed. "Go get him, girlfriend."

I went back up the stairs. As I stood outside Steve's bedroom, my butterfly nerves came back, so I imagined Steve smiling at me and enjoying my company.

I went in, sat down next to him at the computer, did a quick visualization in my head, then turned and gave him a huge smile.

He turned to look at me. "Aaagjjhh. What's the matter with you *now*?"

"Nothing," I beamed, thinking, I am confident, I am great, stunning, brill, dazzling, fantabulous.

Steve looked at me as though I was totally bonkers.

"You're *really* weird, you know that, don't you?" he asked.

Just at that moment, my mobile went.

"'Scuse, Steve," I said as I put the phone to my ear.

"Hey, T. J.," said Scott's voice. "What you doing?"

"Magazine. Remember, I told you. Deadline Monday."

"Oh, that can wait," said Scott. "Wanna go out to the Heath?"

"Sorry, Scott," I said. "Busy. Later."

Then I hung up.

"That guy?" asked Steve.

"That guy."

"And . . .?"

"And . . . history," I said.

Now Steve had a huge grin across his face.

"What's the matter?" I asked.

"Nothing," he beamed.

"You're *really* weird," I said. "You know that, don't you?"

"Yeah," he nodded. "So that makes two of us."

For Real

Summer edition

Contents

Chapter 14

Sabotage

The magazine looked great. We'd done the final layout on Steve's computer, eight full pages that looked fun and interesting.

Steve had found all sorts of visuals on the Internet to liven up the articles, pictures of dogs for the Battersea Dogs' Home article, stars for the horoscope page, herbs and flowers for Izzie's aromatherapy piece. Plus the mad "before" and "after" makeover photographs for the center spread.

It looked good. Very good. I reckoned I was in with a chance.

At assembly on Monday, Mrs. Allen asked that all entries were handed in to our form teacher.

"I know a lot of you have worked very hard on

this," she said, "so we won't keep you waiting. We hope to have an announcement about the winner by the end of the week."

Five minutes later we filed into class and I joined the group hovering around Miss Watkins' desk. I put my copy on the small pile of entries from our class.

"Quite a number getting it all finished on time, wasn't it?" I asked Wendy Roberts, who was standing behind me.

"Er, *no*," she said. "Unlike some saddos in this class, I didn't do one. See, I have a life."

"Oh, I thought you were into it."

"You thought wrong. Deadlines are for losers. And, by the way, Mrs. Allen said she wanted to see you. I saw her just now in the corridor. She wanted you to go to her office immediately."

That's strange, I thought as I hurried off down the corridor to Mrs. Allen's office. I hoped nothing was wrong.

"Mrs. Allen wants to see me," I said as her secretary looked up when I knocked on the office door.

"I don't think so, dear," she said. "Mrs. Allen's in with Mr. Parker. She said not to be disturbed. Must be some mistake."

No mistake, I thought as I went back to class. I suppose Wendy thought she was being funny.

Miss Watkins was at her desk flicking through the entries when I walked back into the class. "You're late, T. J.," she said.

"Er, sorry, miss," I said, going to my desk.

Luckily she didn't go on about it, as Wendy Roberts came in just behind me.

"And you, Roberts, what's your excuse?"

"Loo, miss," she said, breathlessly taking her place.

Miss Watkins continued flicking through the entries. "Well done girls, we have six entries from this class." Then she looked at me. "But I thought we'd have had one more. I thought you were going to enter, T. J."

"I *did*, Miss," I said. "I put it in the pile after assembly."

"Well, it's not here now," she said.

I looked round at Wendy Roberts. She was gazing out of the window, looking like butter wouldn't melt in her mouth.

"Are you sure, T. J.?" said Miss Watkins. "Check your bag."

I did as I was told, but I was sure I'd put it on the desk. "Not there, miss."

"So where is it?"

Suddenly I didn't know what to say. And I had no proof that Wendy had taken it.

"Maybe it's fallen on the floor?"

Miss Watkins had a quick look around, then faced the class.

"Has anyone taken T. J.'s entry?"

No one spoke.

"This is very serious. If T. J. says she put her entry on the pile then either she's lying or someone's taken it. Is anyone going to enlighten me?"

Again no one spoke.

"She *did* do an entry," said Lucy. "I saw it. Honest, miss."

Miss Watkins looked upset. "This is *very* unfortunate, girls. It's almost the end of term and next year, you'll be going into Year Ten. You're not beginners anymore and, frankly, I'm disappointed in this sort of behavior. However, I'm going to ask you to act like mature adults and sort this out amongst yourselves. Twelve thirty this lunchtime is the deadline for entries, so unless you find it, T. J., or someone owns up, I'm afraid there's not a lot more I'm prepared to do."

"That cow," said Lucy, as we filed out at break-time. "I'm sure it was Wendy Roberts."

"Did anyone see anything?" I asked.

Nesta shook her head. "She must have taken it from Miss Watkins's desk when you went to see Mrs. Allen."

"There was a whole crowd round Miss Watkins' desk," said Izzie. "Anyone could have taken it. You know how competitive everyone's been."

"But Wendy did come in after you, T. J. You know, before lessons started. Remember?" said Izzie.

"To the loos," said Nesta. "Let's go."

We ran down the corridor to the cloakrooms. Lucy looked in the cubicles while Nesta searched in the trash can.

"Er*lack*," said Nesta, as she rummaged around amongst bits of old tissue and paper towels.

"Oh, *noooo*," I heard Lucy say, as she reached the third cubicle.

She came out holding a sopping wet pile of ripped paper. "I'm *so* sorry, T.J., it was in the trash can next to the loo."

Izzie took what was left of the magazine. "It looks like she ran it under the tap first."

"But *why*?" I said. "Why has she got it in for me?"

"Doesn't have to be a reason," sighed Nesta. "Some people are just very *very* sad. They can't stand to see anyone else doing well."

"I reckon she never got over being made to look an idiot when Sam Denham was here," said Izzie. "You know, when he praised your answer and dismissed hers."

"What are we going to do?" I said, leaning back against one of the sinks. "I can't hand it in like this."

"We could go to Mrs. Allen," said Nesta.

I was gutted. "We could, but what will that achieve? Only make Wendy hate me more. The main thing is, my entry's unreadable. *All* that work, wasted." I was near to tears. "And all your contributions."

Lucy got her mobile out of her bag. "What time is it?" she said.

"Eleven," I said.

She began dialing frantically.

"Who are you phoning?" I asked.

"Steve," she said. "His year's doing exams and stuff, so their schedule's all over the place.

He might be at home revising."

"Brill," said Izzie. "He's got the mag on his computer. It will only take a minute to print out."

"That's if he's there," said Nesta.

Lucy listened as the phone rang, then she grimaced. "Voicemail," she said. "He must be doing something."

"Leave a message anyway," said Izzie. "It's our only chance."

We went back into the next lesson, but I couldn't concentrate. And neither could Nesta, Izzie, or Lucy, by the looks of it.

"If you look at your watch one more time, T. J. Watts," said Mr. Dixon, "I'm going to take it off you. And Lucy Lovering, if whatever you're staring at outside the window is so fascinating, I suggest you go and stand there for the rest of the lesson."

I glanced across at Wendy Roberts. She looked up from her book and smiled smugly.

You just wait, Wendy Roberts, I thought. It's not over yet.

We flew out of the classroom at lunchtime and out into the playground toward the gates.

No one there.

Lucy got out her phone again. She dialed, then shook her head. "Still on voicemail."

I checked my watch. Ten past twelve.

Twelve fifteen.

Twelve twenty.

"Did you say what time the deadline was when you left the message?" asked Nesta, looking up and down the street anxiously.

"Yeah," said Lucy. "I said twelve thirty. I'll try ringing again."

She was about to dial when Izzie grabbed my arm.

"Here he is," she cried as Steve came flying round the corner on his bike.

He screeched to a stop and pulled an envelope out of his rucksack.

"Good luck," he said as he handed it over.

"Thanks," I called over my shoulder as I ran back inside.

This time I wasn't taking any chances.

I went straight to the staff room and asked for Miss Watkins. I wanted to put my magazine into her hands myself.

Chapter 15

Result

"And the new editor will be . . . ," said Mrs. Allen, as we stood in assembly on Friday.

I held my breath as Nesta gave me the thumbs-up.

"Before I announce the winner, I must say it's been very difficult," continued Mrs. Allen. "The standard of entries was exceptionally high and I'm very proud of all of you. Ultimately there are no losers. We've had a very hard time deciding and . . ."

Izzie gave me a look as if to say, "I wish she'd get on with it."

"Finally we narrowed it down to two. We decided on a tie. Two winners. First, Emma Ford from Year Ten. And second, T. J. Watts from Year Nine."

There were cheers from Nesta, Izzie, and Lucy at the back of the class. But, best of all, Wendy Roberts' face was a picture. Her mouth literally dropped open.

I gave her a huge smile as I went up to join Emma on the stage with Mrs. Allen.

After school we all piled back to Lucy's for celebratory ice cream and cake. When the girls were settled chomping away, Steve beckoned me up to his room.

"I . . . I have something for you," he said shyly.

He went to a drawer in the cabinet next to his bed. He pulled out a small package wrapped in silver, with a gold bow and a card and handed them to me. "These are for you."

I opened the card first. On the front it had a black-and-white photograph of a man on a road, with a caption underneath saying, "Life shrinks or expands in proportion to one's courage." Inside he'd written, "Good Luck to the new Editor of *For Real.*"

"Thanks. That's really . . ."

"Open the pressie," he said, smiling.

I ripped off the paper and found a beautiful pen inside. It was Indian-looking, shiny turquoise and silver with sequinny things on the side.

"Yu . . . nu . . . wee," I said, slipping back into Zoganese for a moment.

"You're welcome," he said, as if he understood perfectly. "It's for writing your novels."

For a moment, we just stayed looking at each other. It was the most perfect feeling. Like time stopped still and we were somehow melting into each other.

Then Steve grinned. "So next . . . ?"

"Next?" I asked. "What do you mean? Next?"

"That day in the park, when you asked how does anyone ever get together and you said for you, they'd have to make it *really* obvious—pressies, cards, a billboard in Piccadilly . . ."

I looked at my card and my present and smiled. "Oh. But please, no, not a billboard in Piccadilly, I'd *die.* . . ."

Steve laughed, then leaned toward me, pushed a lock of hair away from my face, looked deeply into my eyes and . . .

"We could go and see a movie next," he said.

"Love to," I said. "As long as it's not *Alien Mutants in Cyberspace*. And you don't spend the whole movie eating popcorn."

"Deal. Anyway, I hate popcorn."

We sort of grinned stupidly at each other, then I remembered what he'd said that day in the park. That he sometimes felt scared when he liked a girl.

No time like the present, I thought, as I leaned in and kissed him softly on the lips.

e-mail:	Inbox (1)
From:	paulwatts@worldnet.com
To:	babewithbrains@psnet.co.uk
Date:	5 July
Subject:	hol

Dear T. J.

New passport received this morning.
Coming home.

Paul

```
e-mail:      Outbox (1)
To:          hannahnutter@fastmail.com
From:        babewithbrains@psnet.co.uk
Date:        5 July
Subject:     mates, dates
```

Hey Hannahnutter

Whassup? Sorry I haven't been in touch; it's been mad here. So much has been happening. Paul's coming home. Scott is history. Got a date with Steve. Realized boys can be mates as well as dates. Der. Took me a while!

Velly happy. Hope you are.

And I won the competition with Emma Ford from Year Ten. I am now the new joint-editor of the school magazine. Hurrah.

T. J.
XXXXXXXXXXXXXXXXXXXXXXXXXXXXXXXXXXXXX

```
e-mail:      Inbox (1)
From:        hannahnutter@fastmail.com
To:          babewithbrains@psnet.co.uk
Date:        5 July
Subject:     Goody flobbalots
```

Velly solly me no been in touch either.

Goody flobbalots and hurrah about mag thing. I knew you'd get it.

And coolerooney about Steve. I could tell even from a zillion trillion miles away that something was going to 'appen zere. Hasta la banana and many jolly jollities to him. He soundeth superbio. A mate and a date. Best kind.

Mad here too. Replaced ze Luke with ze Ryan. So many boys, so little time etc, etc. Most excellent fun here. Loadsa big bashes and barbies, though I truly miss you and your strange angle on life and SOH.

Send me photos of your new look. And new boy. And new mag.

At last le T. J. has recognized she is ze babe *avec* ze brain.

Keep buzy and yabberyabber spoon.

Lurve and keesses

Your friend for ever and ever and ever and ever and ever and ever and . . . (oh, shutup H)

CHECK OUT AN EXCERPT FROM THE GANG'S

NEXT ADVENTURE!

MATES, DATES, AND Sole Survivors

BY CATHY HOPKINS

Summer
Hols

"This has to be the best feeling in the world," I said to Nesta as we walked out of the school gates on the last day of term.

"I know," she said. "Six weeks with no Miss Watkins. . . . Six fabola weeks with Simon before he goes off to uni."

"And six weeks with Ben for me," said Izzie linking her arm with Nesta's. "We're going to work on loads of new songs for the band now we'll have time."

"And I suppose we'll be seeing *you* round at ours a fair bit," I said to T. J. She's been seeing my elder brother Steve over the last few weeks and they're both completely smitten.

"What about you, Lucy?" asked Nesta. "Going to give *my* poor brother a break at last? You've been giving him the runaround for months now. I don't think his ego can stand much more of it."

Six weeks with Tony? The idea was appealing and I reckoned I was finally ready for a "proper" relationship with him. We'd liked each other for ages and we had gone out for a while earlier in the year, but then I broke it off as it felt like it was all happening too fast. After that there was a lot of flirting between us whenever I saw him round at Nesta's and he did ask me out again a few times, but I turned him down. It's not that I didn't want to date him. He is gorgeous and funny and I love his company, it's just that he has A Bit Of A Reputation when it comes to girls. Nesta had warned me that it was a different one every week at one time. She says he likes the chase, then drops them the minute they show they're interested. So I had to play it carefully, or else by now, I'd be on his long list of rejects and broken hearts. But it had been almost nine months since I met him and he did keep trying, saying I was the only one for him, the lurve of his life. I thought, I can trust him not to mess me about.

I grinned and pulled an envelope out of my rucksack. "I know," I said. "I've been doing a lot of thinking about him lately. And I've finally come to a decision."

"Which is?" asked Nesta.

"I've written him a card. Saying no more messing him about. I really like him and we're on on ON."

"About time," said T. J. "I don't know how you've been so cool for so long. I think I'd have fallen at his feet the first time he asked me out." Then her face clouded. "Um, that is, er, I don't mean I would steal him or anything, I'm just saying I think he's gorgeous."

I squeezed her arm. "I know what you mean, T. J. But boys like Tony enjoy a challenge."

"Well, what is it?" she said. "Eight . . . nine months you've made him suffer? I reckon that's enough challenge for any boy."

"I can hardly believe it," said Izzie. "Last year, none of us had boyfriends. Now this year, we all have."

"It's not definite yet," I said.

"This time last year, I hadn't even been kissed," said T. J.

"And now there's no stopping you," teased Nesta. "Snog Queen of North London."

This time last year, I hadn't been kissed either. Tony was my first. That's another reason I wanted to take it slow. I didn't want to get tied to the first boy I'd snogged. I wanted to try a few others and see what they were like. There have been a few others now. No one important or serious. In fact, no one who's come close to Tony. He still has the same effect on me every time I see him. My stomach turns over and I get all hot and my face goes pink.

"You're not just doing this because you'd be the odd one out?" asked Izzie, pointing at my letter.

"But I *am* the odd one out," I teased. "You're all tall and dark with long hair, and I'm small and blond with short hair."

"No. *I'm* the odd one out," insisted Nesta. "I'm the only one with dark skin."

"No, I'm the——," started T. J.

"I *meant* the only one without a boy," interrupted Izzie.

"No, course not," I said. "I think I'm ready now and I want to see where it goes. To tell the truth, I started thinking that maybe I was messing him around and playing him along because I was scared of rejection. You know what he's like . . ."

Izzie nodded. "Yeah, and you're right. You can't let fear hold you back."

"I've been reading this book," said T. J. "It's by this guy called D. H. Lawrence and it's about a posh lady who falls for her gardener."

"Oh, Mills and Boon?" asked Nesta.

I laughed. Typical Nesta. Her idea of reading is flipping through *Bliss* or *Now* magazine. T. J., on the other hand, T. J. devours books—proper books. That's why she gets on with my brother Steve. He's a bit of a brainbox as well.

"Um, no, not Mills and Boon," said T. J., "but it is a love story. *Lady Chatterley's Lover*, it's called. Anyway there's one line I really like. Want to hear it?"

We all nodded.

"I can't remember it exactly," she said, "as I didn't write it down, but it's something like: better a life of risk and chance than an old age of vain regret."

"Yeah, cool," said Nesta. "I'll buy that. You don't get anywhere in life unless you go for it."

"Feel the fear and do it anyway," said Izzie, quoting the title of one of the self-help books she loves so much.

"So what did you say in the card?" asked Nesta.

"That's Lucy's private business," said Izzie, "Don't be so nosy."

Nesta looked offended and poked her tongue out at Izzie. "I wasn't. I was feeling the fear and asking my question. You don't find out anything if you don't ask what you want to know. So . . .

go on, Lucy, tell us what you said."

I knew the note off by heart, because I'd written and rewritten it so many times. I wanted it to sound right—cool but romantic, so he could keep it as a memento to look back on.

"I did it like one of those Japanese poems," I said, "you know, the ones with only three lines that we did in English last term. Haikus."

"Bless you," said Nesta.

"*No,*" I said. "The poems. They're called haikus."

"Whatever," said Nesta. "So what did you write in your hiccup?"

"I'm not changing, I'm just rearranging, my life to be with you."

"Ahh," said T. J. "That's really sweet."

"Yeah," said Izzie. "You should come and help the band with our lyrics. So what else did you put?"

"Then I wrote, 'Sorry for messing you about over the last year, but now I'm ready. I know we have something really special and I want to make a go of it. Call me.' I wanted to keep it light, you know?"

"Sounds perfect," said T. J.

I took a deep breath and, as we passed a post box, I popped the card in. "Me and Lady Chatterley. No old age of vain regret for us. I've put a first class stamp on, so he should get it in the morning. Gulp. No going back now."

"It'll be fine," said T. J. "I think you'll make a fab couple and we can all do loads of things together—play tennis, go to movies, it'll be great."

"Okay," said Izzie, "so that's Lucy sorted. But there's more to life than boys. Let's make some other goals for the summer holidays."

Typical Iz. She's always setting herself goals and targets, then insists that we do as well. She says it's important to think about what you want in life, then visualize it happening. I visualized me with Tony having a great time. My first proper relationship. It would be top. No worrying about whether you were going to pull or what boys were going to be where. And, did you really like him and did he really like you? Will he phone or should you phone him? . . . It would be good to be settled for a while. All of us. We could all just enjoy being with each other, hanging out as couples and no one having to worry that anyone was on their own.

"*So?*" said Izzie, looking at us all when we reached the bus stop. There's no arguing with Iz when she's off on one of her Let's-improve-ourselves campaigns. "Come on. Resolutions for the summer hols?"

"Resolutions are for New Year," said Nesta, tossing her hair back. "You make them on January first then give up on them around January tenth."

"Okay, I've got four," I said. "Number One: Hang out with you lot as much as poss. Two: You already know now—Tony *et moi*. Three: Stop blushing."

"I think it's lovely that you blush," said T. J. "It's really sweet."

"Noooo," I said. "It's horrible. I feel so stupid and everyone stares like I'm a kid."

"No one ever really notices," said Izzie. "And Number Four?"

"I'm going to make T-shirts," I said. "Like those ones on sale in Camden Market. You know, the ones with cool slogans on them."

"So what are yours going to say?" asked T. J.

"Don't know yet. I'm going to start collecting good lines over the hols."

Just then the bus came, so all discussion was stopped while we piled on. It felt great to be alive. School was over. The sun was shining. The evenings were light until ten o'clock. I'd finally taken the plunge and mailed my card, and I couldn't wait to get his reaction.

"What's for dinner?" I asked Mum when I got home.

"Tofu burgers, broccoli, and rice," she said, looking up from the counter where she was chopping onions. "Want to give me a hand?"

Yuck, tofu, I thought, as I threw down my rucksack in the hall and went to join her. I wish she'd cook normal stuff sometimes. My dad runs the local health shop, so we always eat what he brings back. I know it's good for you, and you are what you eat, etc., but my secret fantasy is to come home one night and discover it's chicken nuggets, baked beans, and chips. It's funny because the way we eat is *Izzie's* fantasy. She loves health food, tofu and soy and quinoa. Sometimes I think we got the wrong parents. Izzie would love to live here; in fact, she almost does, she comes round so often. Me on the other hand, I like living here, but I'd love to have supper at Nesta's. Her dad's Italian and does the most amazing pasta dishes, and her mum's from the Caribbean and her spicy fish and peas is to die for. Amazingly, Nesta is as thin as a rake. I think if I lived at her house, I'd be enormous, so maybe it's a good thing I have strange parents who make peculiar meals.

Suddenly I thought of a good resolution for the holidays.

"Mum, how about this summer, *I* cook supper a few nights?"

"Sounds good to me," replied Mum, grinning.

"Can I get the ingredients as well?"

"Sure," said Mum.

Just at that moment, the phone rang. "Whatever I want?" I asked as I went into the hall and picked up the receiver.

It was Tony.

"Hi," he said. "What you doing later?"

"Nothing," I said. "Nothing for six whole weeks. School ended today."

I decided not to say anything about the card. I wanted it to be a surprise when he opened it in the morning.

"Fancy meeting up?" he asked. "I wanted to talk to you about something."

"What?"

"Not on the phone. I'll meet you at Raj's in Highgate, say, in half an hour."

"Hold on, I'll just ask Mum," I said, putting my hand over the receiver. "Can I go out for a bit? Promise I won't be late. I'll wash up when I get back."

"How can I refuse when you put it like that?" Mum called back. "I'll put your supper in the oven for you."

"See you in half an hour," I said to Tony.

I put the phone down feeling a rush of anticipation. I knew what he wanted to say. He feels the same way I do and wants to make it definite, I thought, as I dashed upstairs and changed into my jeans and a T-shirt. A slick of lip gloss, a squirt of the Angel perfume the girls got me for my birthday, then I ran out and caught the bus up to Highgate. I felt so excited. As I sat on the bus, I decided that I'd let him say what he wanted to say and I'd be cool about it, like, "Oh, I'll have to think about it." Then tomorrow, he'll get my card and realize that I wanted the same thing as him all along. It was all working out so perfectly.

He was already upstairs at Raj's when I arrived. He was settled in the corner seat reading one of the ancient books they keep stacked on the shelves there. He looked up and smiled as I walked in and, as always when I see him, my stomach did a double flip.

"Had your hair cut," I said.

"It's called a French crop. Like it?"

I nodded. Not many boys can take their hair that short, I thought. You have to have good features and the right-shaped head. Of course Tony had both. Good looks run in his family. Nesta is easily the best-looking girl in our school and Tony is probably the best-looking at his. Dark, with sleepy brown eyes and long lashes.

"Take a pew," he smiled, as I slid in behind the table. I smiled back. We always said that when we went there, as the chairs are all old church pews.

"Want some tea or something cold?"

"A Coke would be good," I said as I looked around. I was glad he'd chosen this place to meet. It's T. J.'s favorite place as well as mine. She says she always feels as though she's in a novel from another era when she comes here as the decor is kind of Bohemian. It's different from all the other cafés in the area—it has its own character, with the pews and heavy wooden tables and bookshelves heaving with interesting books.

"What you reading?" I asked.

Tony pointed at the bookshelves. "Oh, some ancient history book. They have a weird collection here, a real mixture, from cookery to Dickens. All the books look about a hundred years old."

I nodded. "Like the nick-nacks," I said, pointing to a chipped statue of an Indian Maharaja on the corner unit above Tony's head. It had been plonked next to a statue of the Buddha. "In fact, it's a bit like our living room at home with all sorts of junk that doesn't really go together."

"Yeah," said Tony, indicating two brass trumpets that were hanging from the ceiling. "It is a bit mad. But I think that's why I like it."

We spent a few minutes chatting about all the strange ornaments we could see—the Russian dolls and toy ostrich on one shelf, brass flamingos and ceramic elephants on another, the old sepia photographs on the wall mixed in with some framed ink sketches. I felt so comfortable sitting there with him that I thought it would be difficult not to spill the beans about my card and my Decision.

"So, you had something you wanted to say?" I finally asked.

"Er, yeah," said Tony, as the boy behind the counter left his computer and came to take our order. "But first, tell me how you are? Out of school, huh?"

I nodded. "Best feeling in the world."

"So what you going to do with the holidays?"

I knew it. He was going to ask if I'd go out with him.

"Oh, no definite plans," I said, looking into his eyes in what I imagined was a meaningful way. "Got any ideas?"

Tony shrugged. "Not really. That is, um, Lucy . . . How can I put this . . . ?"

I longed to reach out and take his hand, tell him that I knew what he wanted to say and that I felt the same. But Nesta had trained me well. Stay cool. Don't be too easy.

Tony took a deep breath. "Thing is, Luce, well, we've been on and off for ages now and I wanted to get things straight between us. It's not fair on you and it's not fair on me. We've got the holidays ahead of us and it's like a new chapter, for both of us, so . . . so, what I think is that, er . . . maybe we should make a clean slate of it."

"Clean slate? What are you saying?" I didn't understand.

"Well, it's not like we're boyfriend and girlfriend, are we? We never really have been."

"No. No, course not." Was he going to ask me if I *would* be now?

"And I was thinking," Tony continued, "what if,

say, you meet someone this holiday or I meet someone? It's kind of confusing. Our situation, that is . . . me and you. Well, we're not free and we're not really committed."

"No, we're not."

"So, what do you think?" he asked.

"I'm not sure I understand," I said. "Are you saying you want to be committed or that you want to meet someone else?"

Tony shifted awkwardly. "That I want to be free," he said finally.

"You're dumping me?" I blurted.

"No. No, course not, how can I dump you when we were never going out properly?"

"But . . ."

He reached for my hand, but I snatched it away. I felt hurt. Confused.

"Look, Lucy, it's not as though I haven't asked you out in the past, but you always put me off."

"I didn't know how I felt then," I blustered. "It wasn't that I was putting you off, but . . ."

"I'm not dumping you. I'm getting it straight, so we both know where we are. We can still be friends."

Friends? I knew exactly what the "We can still

be friends" line meant. It means, that's it. *Finito*. The end. I didn't want to be *friends* with him. I didn't want to hear about him being *more* than friends with anyone else. I looked across at his wide sensuous mouth. No more snogging that mouth. I felt the back of my eyes sting. I was going to burst into tears, but I didn't want to do it there. For him to see how upset I was. "Got to go," I said, getting up.

"But what about your Coke?" I heard him call as I reached the door and stumbled down the stairs.

"You have it," I muttered over my shoulder. I only had one thought in my head as I rushed home. Got to phone Nesta and get her to catch the postman tomorrow morning before Tony sees that stupid stupid *stupid* card.

MATES, DATES, AND SOLE SURVIVORS

BY CATHY HOPKINS

AVAILABLE FEBRUARY 2004

FROM SIMON PULSE